A LOVE IN NAME ONLY

Written by Ginni Conquest

A Love in Name Only   Copyright @2016 Ginni Conquest

Cover Designer: MG Book Covers

Website: www.Ginniconquest.com

Instagram: gindoll1

Facebook: Ginni Conquest

Available on Amazon.com. You can get the book thru Ginni's website:

click on the link and it will take

you directly to her Amazon book page.

You can email Ginni at: Gindoll2005@yahoo.com

Printed in the United States of America

First printing: May 2016

Finished writing December 2015/ re-writes into May 2016

Acknowledgements:

From a dream I had one night; "A Love in Name Only" became a reality for me. I have to thank JD for her encouragement when I told her about my dream, Jaime (my self-appointed "manager") Nadine, Karen and Linda (my three girlfriends since 7th grade), Elaine, Sheila, Lauren, Brittany, Nicole, Shari, Melinda, who was upset with my first book as she didn't want the story to end; this one is extra long for her. To my Parents; Mom, Dad, Sandy and Jerry, (miss you) and my brothers for their support.

To Earnest: Thank you so very much for organizing my book release party. You have made this woman smile and have tears of happiness that you wanted to do this for me. I'm very grateful.

To other writers that I have reached out to during the writing of these books:

Ahren Sanders: I just love her incredible stories and style; Julie Johnson for giving me my first pointers. I hope I get the chance to meet the both of you at some point so I can personally thank you for your influence.

To Melissa at MG Book Covers for the beautiful cover design work: you've made this process an easy one. Glad you were a part of this first book and look forward to working with you on future ones.

Thank you in advance to Jimmy Kimmel for when he has me as a guest on his show. ☺

A special thank you and love to my husband Bobby, my real life romance story; I know my writing takes time away from each other. Thank you for understanding and indulging me in my quest and dream. You guided me with choosing the cover for this book. You have a great eye for it.

My fur babies Rocky and Sammy who are my Basset Hound companions as they lay by my feet as I write and re-write and to everyone that has been following me and purchased my first book. It's difficult when I finish a book; I feel like I'm going thru a breakup of sorts because I love the characters of the stories but at least they end on a happy, forever, together note. Then I get started on another story and bring those characters to life for you. I can only do this as I have gratitude and love for your support and hope that you will fall in love with "A Love in Name Only" as much as I have enjoyed writing this for you. Enjoy the story and romance of Gregory and Samantha.

Xoxo Ginni

Chapter 1 The Dream

It was a restless night for Samantha Hartley. As Vice-President of Public Relations at Crescendo Steele Publishing in Boston, she felt it had to be the stress of her responsibilities keeping her wide awake into the early morning hours. She was in the middle of reading a manuscript from the publishing house's newest romance writer Carlotta Williams, whose novels dealt with supernatural beings and their human love interests. Carlotta was the rising star among the other authors the firm represents and Samantha's own pet project. She really liked Carlotta and her love crazed stories but had to take a step away from reading her novels. Samantha found that she had a vivid imagination and envisioned the characters as they seemed to come to life right out of the pages. Putting the manuscript away, Samantha thought some wine would relax her so she could get some sleep.

As she poured herself a glass, thoughts about her busy schedule tomorrow at the office went thru her mind. Knowing that the CEO and owner Gregory Steele was arriving at the office did not put her mind at ease. The fact that he rarely comes to town and stays mostly at his estate in Maine made the staff wonder why the visit now. Only a handful of the staff had met him, and of course his assistant, Paul Weathers knew him the best. The only thing Samantha knew about him was that he was single and his voice was so commanding and sexy at the same time. She often caught herself daydreaming about him during their conference call meetings with the senior staff. Several times, her best friend Veronica Tate would kick her under the table if she saw Samantha gazing into space. They both started at the firm together after college and formed a strong friendship. Veronica or Ronni as close friends called her, was the Vice-President of International Sales and was a dynamo at her job. Ronni loved life and possessed a winning personality. She was the type of person that found humor in everything that came her way. Samantha thought of calling her but it was late and the wine was already taking effect. She thought that she would just try to go to sleep. Opening the window a bit to let some cool air into her apartment, she turned off her bedroom light and fell into a deep but restless sleep.

Tossing and turning in her bed, Samantha felt that someone was trying to find her in her dream. "Samantha," whispered a voice from deep inside her mind.

"I know that voice, who are you?" Samantha whispered into the darkness.

A soft caress moved up her bare arm, across her shoulder and lightly touched her neck. The caress paused to touch the jeweled cross at the base of her neck and then moved up to her parted lips. "Who are you?" Samantha whispered again. She tried so hard to open her eyes but couldn't get them to move. She seemed to have no control over any part of her body as she moved her face towards the masculine hand that was exploring the contours of her lips. Parting them, she felt his finger outline the fullness of her bottom lip. Licking his finger, she heard a soft laugh coming from the masculine being.

"I have been with you, watching you, dreaming of this moment," the voice said. Samantha felt the masculine hand as it caressed her cheek and moved back to her neck, settling above her breasts. Samantha felt totally confused yet so alive with this man. Feeling the chain bite into her neck, she felt it give way as her cross was tossed aside.

"Open your eyes Samantha, and see me. Do not be afraid of me or of who I am."

At that moment, the rays of the full moon softly lit up her bedroom. Samantha slowly opened her eyes and saw the most beautiful deep brown eyes that she has ever seen in a man. Sensual lips, dark wavy hair and a muscular, strong chest all attacked her senses; she didn't know what to do. Was this really happening or was she imagining all of this?

"Samantha, you need to come freely to me. I can't take you against your will."

Samantha felt herself reaching out to this mystery man and brought his face down to hers for a kiss that she never experienced in her lifetime. Her very essence was being given to this dream maker, this phantom, this almost perfect man. His mouth left hers and trailed to the pulse beating wildly in her neck. Feeling his lips and tongue touching a tender spot, Samantha didn't care who he was. She just knew that only he would be the one to satisfy the need growing inside of her. Feeling him move against her hip, she let a soft moan escape her lips as she exposed the sexy curve of her neck to him.

"Samantha, I want you to look into my eyes when I take some of your life from you."

At that point, she looked at him in disbelief as she felt his teeth bite into her neck.

"No!" She cried out and sat up panting in her bed. Reaching for the light, she turned it on and looked next to her. No one was there. It was that moment of being in a dream and a waking state that Samantha wasn't quite sure what just happened. As she felt her heart beating wildly in her chest, she grabbed for her neck and it felt tender to her touch.

Jumping out of bed, Samantha ran to the mirror to look at herself. "What is happening?" There were two tiny cuts and some little scratches showing up on her neck. "Where is my necklace?" Stepping on something on the floor, she bent down and found where her cross was laying. Holding it close to her, Samantha started trembling as she looked back into the mirror. She must have pulled the necklace off during this dream and cut herself. That would be the perfect explanation. Being totally confused over what she experienced, Samantha just stood still trying to analyze what happened. She didn't see anyone in her room or hear anyone in her apartment. Taking deep breaths to calm down, she started looking around in each room. Nothing was out of place and there wasn't anyone in her apartment. Going back into the bedroom, she locked her door and closed the window. Gazing at her alarm clock, she saw it was 5 o'clock in the morning. Where did the night go? Samantha decided to take a hot shower and get ready for work as she knew that sleep would evade her. Waiting for the hot water to come on, she couldn't help but think about that voice and that she had heard it somewhere before. How could this dream make her feel so alive? Stepping into the shower, Samantha caressed her body while she imagined it was his hands touching her, exploring her and loving her.

One thing was for certain, she never felt so alive and aroused at the same time. She blamed Carlotta and her damned supernatural romance novel for this experience. Thought for the rest of the week: do not read Carlotta's books before going to sleep.

Toweling herself dry, Samantha knew that it would do her some good to get to the office early to tackle some work. She also wanted to catch Ronni to speak to her about the dream as she felt compelled to tell someone about it. Why not talk to Ronni about this? I could use some of her humor at this time thought Samantha. Pulling her chestnut waves into her usual ponytail for work, she decided not to wear it up but to wear it down today. She just felt different, her life felt different. Gazing into the mirror, Samantha was satisfied with how she looked in her skirt, blouse and jacket. Finding a scarf to tie around her neck to cover the cuts and scratches there, Samantha was ready to face the CEO and find out why he decided to be in town now of all days. She had no idea that today was going to change her entire life. Making sure that everything was locked up and in its place, Samantha grabbed her handbag and leather case as she headed over to the corner deli for her usual green tea before going to the office.

Chapter 2   The Proposition

Arriving at the office, Samantha noticed she wasn't the only one getting a head start today with the CEO coming to town. Her assistant Cindy was already there placing Samantha's schedule on her desk. Cindy has been her trusted assistant from day one at her job. They both worked together as a team and not just as a boss and an assistant. Cindy loved working with Samantha as she found her to be very fair, respectful and easy going.

"Good morning Samantha, you look different today. It must be your new look with your hair down. I really love it."

"Thanks Cindy. I just felt like doing something different today."

"You should wear it this way more often." Walking over to Samantha, she made a notation of the change in her schedule.

"Here's your new schedule. Paul has changed your meeting with

Mr. Steele to a lunch one, just you and him."

"I wonder what that change is all about," Samantha said. Not given a chance to think further about that change, a sassy blonde put her head around the door. Ronni was her over the top self this morning. "Well good morning you sexy thing you! I love your hair down and you have a glow about you. What did you do last night?"

"Thanks Cindy," said Samantha. Cindy closed the office door behind her. Samantha turned towards Ronni and leaned back against her desk.

"Ronni, I had the most amazing, yet crazy dream last night. It seemed so real that I just don't understand it." Samantha felt almost embarrassed to tell Ronni about it.

"Well do tell Sam," Ronni said. "I could use some excitement in my life. Was it really a hot one?" "I'm almost embarrassed to tell you but I have to tell someone," Samantha said. "It just wasn't what he did but it was his voice. He said that I had to come to him willingly and that he couldn't take me against my will. I had to look into his eyes while he takes a part of my life from me. Then he kissed me and started to bite my neck."

Ronni just stared at Samantha and started laughing.

"Does he have a brother? He sounds wonderful but I think you are reading too many of your new author's novels, especially before you go to sleep."

"That's what I thought too but does this look like I dreamed this up?" She took the scarf off her neck to show Ronni.

"Ok so now you think are dreaming of what, a vampire? Was he a sensuous man? Was he sexy like Frank Langella's Dracula or even like that gorgeous Gerard Butler's portrayal of Dracula?"

"I'm serious Ronni, I never felt this alive as during that dream but I knew the voice. He was so ruggedly handsome and those eyes. One could get lost in them."

"Ok," Ronni said. She jumped up and grabbed a pen and paper.

"It's time that you become a hot romance author. You should write all of this down as you will make a fortune. Women will pay big bucks to read this kind of stuff, including me!"

"Ok, you aren't taking me seriously and now I have to get thru my morning schedule before my lunch meeting with Mr. Steele. I'll talk to you later, now go on and get out of here," Samantha laughed.

"Sure thing. Enjoy your thoughts about your new mystery dream lover and let me know how lunch goes. Maybe the boss wants to give you a new position so call me later."

"We're still on for dinner, right?"

"Yep, looking forward to it," answered Ronni.

Samantha sat down deep in thought, her hand absently touching her neck. This is ridiculous thought Samantha. Ronni was right. It was just a dream, nothing else and with that, Samantha got thru her morning work. It was nearing her lunch meeting with CEO Gregory

Steele that Samantha found herself stuck on a conference call. Without realizing that someone was standing in her doorway watching her, Gregory Steele stood motionless while observing everything about Samantha.

The sunlight was striking Samantha's chestnut waves making her seem almost ethereal and untouchable at the same time. From the button down silk blouse that clung to her curves, to the black pencil skirt right down to her slim legs and two inch heels, Gregory Steele just stared at the vision in front of him without being noticed.

"I have Carlotta set up for several book signings on the west coast, including LA, San Diego and especially San Fran. Her sales are thru the roof there so we'll make the most of her appearances in that city. Just get the publicity packages out to the various venues that I'm emailing to you right now and get the hotels set up for her with a driver in each city. Carlotta is one of our successful up and coming authors and will be treated as such," Samantha said to her counterpart on the west coast. Sensing someone was watching her, she said goodbye and turned to look at the door.

"Nicely done Ms. Hartley, I'm Gregory Steele."

Grabbing onto the edge of her desk, Samantha felt very light headed and didn't know if her legs were going to support her. Running over to her, Gregory caught Samantha before she touched the floor. Her assistant Cindy chose that very minute to witness everything.

"I'll get some water and a cool cloth Mr. Steele," as she ran off. Samantha slowly regained her composure and looked at the man in her dream.

"It's you," she whispered. Gregory smirked down at her but didn't say anything as Cindy ran back into the room.

"Here you go Mr. Steele, Samantha are you ok?"

"She will be fine Cindy, thank you for your concern. I'll take care of Ms. Hartley now," Gregory said. Being dismissed, Cindy closed the office door as Gregory effortlessly picked up Samantha and placed her on the couch. Sitting down next to her, Gregory was searching her face to make sure she was recovering. Pushing a stray curl from her face, he looked down at her with concern and also with puzzlement.

"What did you mean when you said to me "it's you"?" Gregory asked.

"I'm sorry Mr. Steele for almost fainting; it's not like me to be startled like this. You look so much like someone I know," Samantha said. She was going to add from her dream but didn't want to sound like a lunatic to her boss. She couldn't take her eyes off of his handsome face, the face of her dream. This is pure coincidence and can't be happening thought Samantha.

"I didn't realize that I had this effect on women Ms. Hartley, you flatter me," Gregory said. "Let's chalk it up that you have been working hard all morning, probably didn't eat breakfast or a snack and maybe a bit nervous about what our lunch meeting is all about. Then I showed up unannounced and now you are in my arms."

"Now you sound like one of our writers, Mr. Steele, a bit of a romantic yourself perhaps?"

"We'll see over lunch if you would classify me as such. Are you feeling better to still go?"

"Yes, let me grab my bag and give Cindy a few things to get done for me. I'll be ready in a few minutes." As Gregory reached down to help her up from the couch, he held her in his arms a bit longer than necessary. Samantha just looked into his eyes as her lips parted in response to his gaze at her mouth. Running her tongue over her bottom lip, Gregory tightened his grip on her arms that was noticeable by Samantha. Raising his eyes to hers, she felt that he was just about to say something to her when the office door slammed open. Ronnie barged into the room after she heard about her friend. Releasing Samantha's arms, Gregory continued to stand close to her in case she felt faint again.

"I heard you passed out in front of Mr. Steele. Are you ok?" She was so concerned about Samantha that she really didn't focus on Gregory standing in the room.

"Um Ronni, let me introduce you to Mr. Steele." Gregory came over to Ronni with his hand extended to greet her. For once, Ronni was speechless. What a handsome man she thought. No wonder Samantha almost fainted when she met him. I would need mouth to mouth if this happened to me.

"It's a pleasure to meet you Ms. Tate. I've done extensive research on the work each of my employees does at this firm and I am very pleased with the work you are doing."

"Thank you Mr. Steele. Ok Sam, I have to run. See you later at dinner."

Samantha frowned as she watched the door close. Now that was very strange behavior for Ronni. It was though she couldn't wait to get out of the room. She caught Gregory staring intently at her which shook her out of her thoughts.

"Let me speak to Cindy and I'll be ready to leave," Samantha said. "Meet me down the hall at Paul's desk when you're ready," said Gregory and was gone. Samantha caught herself thinking about Mr. Steele. Not a great way to meet your boss by nearly fainting at his feet. He looks so much like the man in my dreams and that voice. It was him but how? I've never met him before.

After giving Cindy some added instructions for Carlotta's book tour, she touched up her lipstick, made sure her scarf was in place to cover the scratches and went in search of Mr. Steele.

Approaching the CEO's office, Samantha noticed the ever faithful Paul Weathers at his post outside of Mr. Steele's office. He was a very nice distinguished man, who at one time worked for Samantha's Aunt Elaine at the advertising firm she had owned. Loyal to a fault, Paul was one that was always trusted and maintained positions near the top of the business world. Any CEO would be privileged to have Paul working by their side.

"Greetings Ms. Hartley," said Paul. "Mr. Steele asked you to please wait here; he'll be right with you. I heard you fainted when you met him and I trust that you are feeling better."

"I didn't actually faint. Remind me to give Cindy triple the amount of work for talking about this," murmured Samantha.

"She was just concerned about you Ms. Hartley, we all were. I have to say that's the first time I've heard that a woman has passed out in Mr. Steele's arms."

"I guess I'll never live this down," Samantha said.

"Hardly unlikely," answered Paul with a sassy smile.

At that moment, Gregory came out of his office. Happy to see that Samantha was there, they needed to get going to keep their reservation at the restaurant.

"Are you ready?"

"Yes, all set," answered Samantha. Gregory held the elevator door for her. It was a quiet ride between the two of them. She was so deeply aware of the sensuality of him that she couldn't remember ever being attracted to a man like this before. The main floor couldn't have come fast enough as she needed to get out of this closed up space with him. What does one say to a CEO to make small talk? Talking about the weather would be a lame choice thought Samantha so she thought she would remain silent until he

divulged what this lunch meeting was all about. Once outside,
Gregory escorted her to his black Maserati parked in a space
reserved just for him. The car had a dangerous look about it, just
like its owner. Of course he would handle a car like this. It suited
him. He opened the door for her, waited for her to settle herself in
and closed it with her safely tucked in its seat. The car smelled of a
mixture of leather and his cologne, very masculine. Samantha tried
to bring herself out of this mood; this is a business lunch, this dream
was an illusion and this man is your boss who can fire you at any
given moment.

His door opening stopped her from her daydreaming. Now this was
time for work.

As the car started with a purr of an engine, Samantha couldn't take
her eyes off the masculine hand that was shifting gears.
Samantha forced herself to look away as she heard the slight
chuckle coming from Mr. Steele.

"So Samantha, may I call you Samantha?" Not trusting herself to
speak at that moment, she just nodded at him. Giving her a
boyishly handsome smile, she couldn't help but wonder how his lips
and teeth would feel on her skin. She tried to remain focused on
what he was saying to her.

"Ok Samantha. I want you to please call me Gregory or Greg,
whichever you prefer. I think we have surpassed all formalities since
you have already fainted in my arms." He was clearly enjoying her

embarrassment of the situation. She noticed the smirk that caught on the corner of his lips.

"Ok Mr., I mean Gregory. Where are we going?"

"We are going to my favorite cafe in a quiet part of town. I don't want to be interrupted or distracted while having lunch with you. We should be there in a few moments. I'm sure Paul has our reservation all set. I have a business proposition to discuss with you that I'm hoping you will agree to as I need someone like you to get the job done," explained Gregory.

"Now you have my interest Gregory."

"I thought I had your interest when you first saw me," Gregory replied. A little somersault turned in the pit of Samantha's stomach. Feeling her face turn a nice shade of pink, Samantha looked out the window as Gregory was pulling the car into a parking space with ease. Shutting the car off, he turned her face to him. Reaching up to touch her cheek, he brushed a piece of her hair behind her ear.

"Pink becomes you," he whispered. Gregory climbed out of his car and walked to her side to help her out. Thoroughly confused as to what this lunch is about, the flirting didn't seem like proper office protocol, especially coming from a CEO. Samantha figured she would find out soon enough. Reaching down with his hand, she placed hers in his as he gently guided her out of the car. He looked at her shapely leg that she placed on the street and how her skirt and blouse molded her figure. Before he let go of her hand, she felt his thumb caress her palm which sent shivers right through her body. With a slight smile on his face, he opened the restaurant door for her and they entered the foyer. He knows the effect he has on me thought Samantha.

"Good afternoon Mr. Steele," said the hostess. "It's nice of you to come back and visit us. Your table is in the corner overlooking the gardens as requested."

"Thank you," Gregory said.

Being the complete gentleman she knew he would be, Gregory held Samantha's chair for her. Within seconds, their waiter brought over a bottle of red wine, Gregory's favorite. He must come here often when he's in town Samantha thought. As if reading her mind, Gregory poured some of the wine for her.

"This is my favorite place when I come to town. The food is incredible and the service is the best. I recommend anything on the menu."

Samantha thought that anything she would eat right now would taste like a piece of cardboard anyway so it really didn't matter. What was this lunch about? The thought was driving her crazy.

"I could order for you if you like," Gregory said.

Without waiting for her answer, he took charge of their lunch order starting with fresh scallops, followed with grilled salmon and assorted spring vegetables and fresh berries with their homemade signature ice cream for dessert.

"My downfall," said Gregory.

"Mine too," agreed Samantha.

As they started to enjoy their lunch, Samantha was a bit more relaxed as she finished her first glass of wine. Feeling stronger to deal with whatever Gregory wanted to speak to her about, Samantha just came out with her question.

"So Gregory, what is the business proposition you wanted to speak to me about?"

Without missing a beat, he put his fork down.

"I need a wife," Gregory said.

"Excuse me, what did you say?"

"I need a wife Samantha," said Gregory. Sensing she was going to interrupt him, Gregory put up one of his hands to continue his story. "Let me explain. I'm working on several merging aspects of my business with foreign companies and well, it would look better and more secure to those at the companies if I had a wife; as in more stability, a family life. I have spent my life building this company that I haven't had the time or the need to have serious relationships. Don't get me wrong, I've had my share of that kind of a relationship but no one I've dated was someone I wanted as a my partner in life. You are the perfect match for this job, you are savvy at this business and an attractive, smart woman," Gregory said. He stopped for a moment to let his offer sink in.

"Here is what I'm offering to you. For one year, as that's how long I feel it will take for the mergers to complete, you will still work in your position in my company.

I will give you a very generous allowance every month plus pay for your apartment in the city so you have it when our year is up. You will need a whole new wardrobe that I will purchase for you, especially for entertaining. You will be expected to live with me at my apartment as well as my estate in Maine when I'm there. You will have your own bedroom suite at both places. If you decide to change the sleeping arrangements to my bedroom, I certainly would not object to that." Picking up his wine glass, he took a sip while looking right into her eyes to make his point. Samantha couldn't look away from him; his gaze held her captive while her heart was racing at the sexual tension that was in the air between them. Placing the glass down, he continued with his offer. "After a year, I will grant you a divorce and you will be well compensated for your sacrifices for the year."

Samantha knew she looked dumbfounded as she asked, "Why me?"

"I've discussed this at length with Paul and you were the first and only person he knew that could do this. He knows you are unattached right now and said you have a good character background. He just didn't tell me how beautiful you are. I hope you don't mind me saying that," Gregory said. He looked at her incredulous expression as she tried to decipher exactly what was happening here.

"Please consider this proposition. You will become a wealthy woman after the year is over but there is one thing I won't tolerate. We will be married and have to portray the happy in love couple. Neither one of us will entertain anyone else in our life for the duration of the year. I will have a contract drawn up by an outside attorney not connected with this business. I'm asking you to seriously consider this proposition."

Samantha's mind was going in circles. Be married in name only to this man? Am I really seriously considering this proposal? Gregory was watching her intently.

"You don't have to give me an answer now but by the end of the week would suffice."

When their lunch came to the table, Gregory changed the subject to what was happening in her department as he wanted to get up to speed with their clients. Watching Samantha talk about her part of his business, she was animated with excitement as she described each author. She lived for this business and Gregory thought he couldn't have chosen a more perfect woman for this job. He hoped that she would accept his offer. As their lunch continued, Gregory couldn't help but notice that he was attracted to her. This wasn't something that he was expecting. It was almost better if he wasn't attracted to her. She could be too much of a distraction for the work that he needed to accomplish. They both settled into a comfortable mood and enjoyed each other's company. Samantha asked him about the goals for his business and he shared with her his dream of expanding the business into the European market.

"That's why I am asking you to be my wife Samantha." As Gregory signed the check, Samantha gathered her bag and waited for him at the front of the restaurant. This was definitely not the proposition she thought would be offered to her. Let me punch Paul when I see him for recommending me. But would this be so bad? Am I really considering this?

"Ready?" He opened the door for her and they walked to the car together. He reached for her hand on the way to the car.

"See, not so bad Samantha. This could be the perfect arrangement." He slowly lowered his lips to her cheek. "Thank you for meeting me for lunch and for considering this proposition." He helped her into the car and got in behind the wheel. They both sat in silence on the drive back to the office. Samantha was processing everything that he offered her. It definitely wasn't something that she thought her lunch was going to be. Dropping her off at the front entrance of the company, she thanked him for a very interesting lunch.

"Nice to see you have a sense of humor too. I'll check in with you later," Gregory said.

Samantha walked numbly thru the doors into the elevator. Pressing the button to her floor, she went thru the whole conversation in her mind. Being his wife in name only; how long would that last?

Getting off on her floor, Samantha realized that Carlotta Williams had an appointment with her and she was already few minutes late meeting her.

Chapter 3 Consideration

Carlotta was already in the office, passing out herbal teas to the staff. She was a warm woman in her early 60's with a keen imagination. Her books had a flair for the supernatural and were extremely sexy at times. You would never guess these racy books came from a woman that looks like someone's grandmother but that's what made her so much fun to be around. "Samantha, come join our party! I found this new amazing tea house and just had a round delivered to the office with these fresh berry scones." Carlotta came over to Samantha to give her a big motherly hug. "I love how you look with your hair down too. I always see you with your hair up. This is so much more alluring. Maybe I'll use you as a subject in my next book," exclaimed Carlotta.
"Don't you dare," Samantha said. "Your books give me wild dreams."
"Yeah," shouted Ronni from across the table. "Samantha had a wild dream after reading your new book. You should ask her about it." Samantha gave Ronni a look to kill as she blew Samantha a kiss from across the room. Carlotta definitely wanted to hear all about it.
"When my book gives someone a dream, then I know I've written a

good one. Come Samantha, we have to talk about my tour anyway and you can fill me in on this dream of yours."

As Samantha closed her office door, she started explaining the tour stops.

"Stop right there," Carlotta said. "Let's sit for a minute and catch up. You look entirely too flustered when I know you to be a calm and cool woman. What about the dream?"

Taking a deep breath Samantha blurted out everything so quickly because of her embarrassment of it.

"Well, I dreamt about a gorgeous, sensual man that came to me the other night. He was a vampire like character and he was my boss Gregory." Carlotta intently looked at Samantha. Waiting for Carlotta to start laughing, just the opposite happened.

"Of course he was Gregory Steele. Don't you remember that about 8 months ago when I started writing the outline for the book, I heard thru the grapevine how handsome Gregory was so I Googled him. And they were so right! He was the perfect leading man for my book. I had brought in photos to show you so that's why you dreamt of him. I can assure you though, he isn't a vampire. A sexy man, Hell yes," Carlotta said. Samantha still looked pensive. "What's the matter Samantha?" Looking at Carlotta, Samantha started with the other part of the story.

"You have to promise me that you won't say anything that I'm going to tell you. As you know, I had a lunch meeting with Gregory today because he offered me a proposition. He asked me to marry him, not for love but a marriage in name only, purely for business so he would look more appealing as a business partner to foreign company owners," explained Samantha. She braced herself for more possible laughter but received a totally different reaction. "You should do it Samantha. What do you have to lose? I'm sure he offered you a sizable amount of money and wonderful perks. Haven't you heard about arranged marriages? This is another form of that, more of a modern age type of arranged marriage." Carlotta reached out for Samantha's hands. "If I may speak to you as a mom, I would love to share some advice to you. It's so difficult to meet a good man nowadays. Here you have an offer, an exciting one I might add, with a handsome, smart man. You are a beautiful, smart woman; you are a good pair together. You have put your heart and soul into his company so you both have the same work ethics. And stranger things have happened in situations like these. Maybe the both of you will fall madly in love, have babies and live happily ever after."

"Now that's my favorite romance author," Samantha said. "Thank you for your advice and I will consider all that you have said. When I think about it, it would be an exciting year."

"And maybe a good loving year too," giggled Carlotta. "Go with your heart, you're already attracted to him, what's the harm? You will have his ring on your finger."

"Ok Carlotta, that's moving a little too fast. Let's get to work on your tour as you will be leaving next week," Samantha said. She reached over to hug Carlotta when there was a knock at the door. Cindy came in carrying a beautiful flower delivery of red roses and left them in front of Samantha. Carlotta raised her eyebrows and waited to hear who they were from but they both knew. Samantha's hand shook slightly as she reached for the card. Opening it, she read it out loud to Carlotta.

"It says "Please say yes! And it's signed with a G," Samantha said.
"Well you know what I would do if I were 30 years younger? To be around that virile a man, I can think of plenty of things and it wouldn't be holding his hand," laughed Carlotta. She pretended to faint as she fanned herself.

"Thanks Carlotta, let's get back to work, shall we?" Two hours later, Carlotta was all set with her itineraries and the promise to keep in touch with Samantha.

"Don't over think things Samantha. Just follow your heart," Carlotta said. Hugging her, Samantha thanked her for her insight and wished her good luck with her tour. Now Samantha knew what she had to do. Finishing up with last minute notes, she said goodnight to Cindy and walked straight to Gregory's office.

"Hi Paul, is he in?" Not waiting for an answer, she barged into Gregory's office. Seeing her, Gregory finished his call as she closed the door. He came around to the front of his desk as she came towards him.

"As your wife, you better get used to me coming into your office like this." Samantha couldn't believe she was going to go thru with this but she was throwing caution to the wind and taking a chapter out of Carlotta's book of living. Gregory reached for her hands and kissed them. "Thank you for agreeing to this. I will have the contract taken care of and purchase a beautiful ring for you. We'll start our wedding plans and work out everything else if agreeable to you," said Gregory.

"Now how do we explain this to the people in this company? They know I've never met you and now I'm walking down the aisle with you," Samantha said.

"It will be a whirlwind romance and you just simply could not live without me," teased Gregory. He reached out to pull her close to him. "We have to show people how attracted we are to each other, but I think you already know this, don't you Sam." It wasn't lost on Samantha that he used her nickname and that his hands were slowly moving across her back, pulling her even closer to him. She placed her hands up and around his neck, feeling his muscles tightening from her touch. It was nice to know that she was having the same effect on him as he was on her.

"I'm going to kiss you now Sam." Samantha took the lead and pulled his face down to hers. Gregory was pleasantly surprised at her first move towards him but took over the kiss, driving her completely crazy with wanting him, teasing her, moving his mouth from hers and kissing her down her throat to find her pulse beating wildly. He slowly moved back up to her mouth as his hand found its way to her breast, lightly caressing her nipple thru her blouse. Samantha knew she had to gain control over her emotions so she slowly stopped kissing him. Pulling her close in front of him, she felt his desire for her thru her skirt. Giving her a slight smile, Gregory touched her cheek as he felt her tremble at his touch. A knock at the door brought them both to their senses. Making sure Samantha was presentable, Gregory acknowledged who was at the door.

"Mr. Steele, am I needed for anything else today?" Paul asked. He discreetly took in the scene before him.

"No that's all for today Paul. Thank you."

"Are congratulations in order sir?" Paul asked.

"Yes Paul," said Gregory. "Samantha and I are getting married, however, we will need your assistance in letting people know that it's been a whirlwind romance and we can't be without each other."

"Well isn't that the truth sir?" Paul said. "I'll say goodnight to both of you and congratulations." As he closed the door, Gregory thought about Paul's comment as he looked over at Samantha. "I'm sorry that we were interrupted while getting to know one another," smiled Gregory.

"I'm going to get going," Samantha said. "I've promised to meet Ronni for dinner so I'm going to go now." She realized she just repeated herself twice and really didn't say things correctly as this man totally unnerved her. Sensing her confusion, Gregory came over to her.

"It will be fine Sam and not entirely uncomfortable as time goes on. I'll call you later." He kissed her lightly on the forehead.

Samantha walked towards the door with as much sophistication that she certainly didn't feel. "Thank you for the beautiful roses too."

Samantha closed his door and stood up against it for a few seconds. She had several relationships in her life but nothing as exciting or as dangerous as Gregory Steele. Now she is getting married to him.

As she walked back to her office, Samantha thought that we have to set boundaries. A kiss like what just happened would have easily escalated into something that she wasn't prepared for. She silently thanked Paul for his perfect timing.

Chapter 4   Friends

Driving to the restaurant, Samantha rehearsed how she was going to explain all of this to Ronni.

She kept thinking about Gregory's kiss. It was totally hot as she remembered her reaction to him. It was though he already branded her as his as she still tasted him on her lips. Running a few minutes late, Samantha finally arrived at the Mayflower Restaurant. She quickly scanned the bar and found Ronni entertaining a few eligible men who seemed to be totally captivated with her. This was so typical of her friend. Samantha wished she could have that free, flirty nature with the opposite sex but she was a bit more serious when it came to affairs of the heart.

"Oh Sam," Ronni called out. "Come and meet my new friends Steve and Charlie."

Samantha heard Gregory's words in her head; neither of us will entertain another person for the year we are together.

"Nice to meet you both," said Samantha politely. "Ronni, our table is ready, would you mind if we go now. There are some things I need to discuss with you."

Ronni got up with a pouty look on her face.

"Sorry guys, it's a girls night out," said Ronni regretfully. "You have my business card, give me a call sometime."

Ronni linked her arm thru Samantha's as they walked to their table.

"I don't know how you do it Ronni," laughed Samantha.

"It's easy. I just turn on the charm and be myself."

"That's why I love you," laughed Samantha.

Relaxing for the first time that day, they sat down by the window overlooking the bay. Samantha reached for a glass of sparkling water that the waiter left on their table for them.

"Put that water down; let's order a bottle of champagne as I'm sure you have something to celebrate after your lunch with our sexy boss." Samantha choked on the water she was drinking.

"What makes you say that Ronni?" Samantha asked.

"Well, I'm guessing he offered you another position as you have been doing an amazing job. You know I'm so proud of you. " Samantha thought this was as good a time as any to let Ronni know her secret.

"Well he did offer me a position which I have accepted. I'm going to be his wife for one year in name only so he has more success in his dealings with the foreign businesses he is working with." Ronni just stared at her unblinking. "Please say something Ronni, even something witty and insane. I need to hear something like that from you," begged Samantha. "I just want to make sure I'm doing the right thing in my life."

"I hope I'm your Maid of Honor," squealed Ronni. "This is so incredible. Do you have to sleep with him? Can you imagine what it would be like with him? That body is to die for. What did you work out with him?"

"He will pay my rent for a year so I'll have my place when our agreement is over. I'll get a stipend every month, not expected to sleep with him but will be expected to live with him at both residences. He will purchase an entire wardrobe as I'll need clothes for entertaining and we can't see anyone else for a year during our marriage. After a year, he will grant me a divorce. This will be a marriage in name only unless I want it to be something more, then he doesn't have an objection to that."

"Well if I was you, I would work on changing that part on the honeymoon," commented Ronni. "Not expected to sleep with him! What is he, a monk or something? Has he taken a good look at you?"

"You think we'll go on a honeymoon?" Samantha heard a little panic creep into her voice. She was stuck on the honeymoon comment.

"Yep," Ronni said. "Hopefully some place hot and romantic! To see that man in his bathing suit or wearing nothing at all, what a fantasy come to life that is!" Ronni motioned over the waiter. "We would love some champagne please. My best friend just got engaged and I'm her Maid of Honor!"

Samantha sat back and smiled. She loved her friend Ronni, could always trust her and knew she would need her during these next months.

"To Samantha and Gregory, the hottest couple in the publishing world. May you both fall madly in love with each other and have lots of babies!"

"That's what Carlotta said. Let's hold up on the second part of your toast."

So they enjoyed a great dinner together planning Samantha's wedding. Ronni was giving her wedding night advice and they were just having fun like their old college years. It was after midnight when Samantha let herself back in her apartment. Hearing her cell phone ringing, she knew who it was without seeing the number.

"Hello," Samantha said.

"How is my fiancé doing? Did you tell Ronni about us?" Samantha felt her insides quiver when she heard Gregory's voice.

"Yes, I did. She is very happy for us and gave me lots of honeymoon advice," Samantha said.

She couldn't believe she just said that to him. It must be the champagne.

"I knew I liked Ronni. What kind of advice did she give you?"

"You will just have to wait and see Mr. Steele," teased Samantha. "I just might have something planned for you."

"I wish I were with you right now so you could give me a trial run," answered Gregory. "But something tells me you have had a little bit too much celebration tonight that's giving you the courage to speak to me like this. You are tempting fate Samantha. I will pick you up at 9 o'clock tomorrow. We have some jewelry shopping to do and an appointment with the lawyer too. I look forward to knowing what you have planned for me. Goodnight Sam. Sweet dreams."

After he hung up, Samantha thought why did I have to talk to him like this? It was like waving a red flag in front of a bull. Feeling a champagne headache coming on as well as wishing Gregory was with her propelled her into the kitchen to grab a few aspirin and a full glass of water. She couldn't believe that she was feeling this way towards Gregory as she just met him. Without another thought, Samantha stripped off her clothes and dove naked under her sheets. She hoped that the cool fabric would calm her feelings down as the last thought before sleep claimed her was Gregory's kiss.

Chapter 5 Shopping

Loud knocking at Samantha's door woke her from a sound sleep. "Oh no," groaned Samantha at the loud pounding. Rolling over she glanced at the clock that showed 9 o'clock, just the time that Gregory said he would pick her up.

"I didn't set my alarm; I can't believe I did this!"

Grabbing her robe, she hurried into the bathroom. Putting her hair up in a pony tail, she quickly brushed her teeth and then ran to the front door. As she opened it, Gregory stood there in black jeans, casual tee-shirt with a denim shirt over that. He looked so amazingly handsome.

"I'm so sorry Gregory. I didn't set my alarm and well had a little bit too much celebrating last night with Ronni," explained Samantha. "Please come in. It won't take me long to get ready and make yourself comfortable. Put on the TV if you want to watch the news or something."

Gregory stood there watching her intently. The top part of her robe had opened a bit, exposing part of the luscious curve of her breast. His eyes caught the sway of her hips as she walked away of him. So she sleeps naked and just looks so adorable in the morning thought Gregory. This year could have many possibilities that he was willing to explore. He only hoped Samantha would want that too or it was going to be a long and lonely year for him.

"Samantha," Gregory said. She stopped to look at him. "Pink becomes you," saying the same thing that he did at the restaurant. This time he referred to her bathrobe but he would much rather have her naked in his arms. His eyes relayed those feelings to Samantha so she moved quickly to her bedroom and shut the door. Turning on the shower as hot as she could stand it, Samantha stood under the spray as she cleared her mind from the last effects of the champagne but couldn't rid herself of her feelings about Gregory. This wasn't like her at all. She just met him, agreed to marry him and now was thinking of all kinds of other things with him. "I'm losing my mind," thought Samantha. Jumping out of the shower, she got ready in record time. After drying her hair, she just added some mascara to her lashes to bring out her blue eyes and added some lip gloss. She brushed her waves and decided to leave her hair down again. She ran in her closet for her favorite pair of boyfriend jeans and a pair of soft flats. Adding a tee-shirt and a simple necklace, she followed Gregory's lead with similar attire. Grabbing her bag, she was ready to go.

Heading back over to where Gregory was waiting, he appreciated her simple, classy style. Reaching out for her hand, he pulled her to him.

"I want to give you a proper good morning hello," Gregory said. He tipped her mouth up to his and captured it with a force that even surprised him. There was just something about this woman that he wanted to protect and take advantage of at the same time. He was encouraged that she met his kiss with a passion that matched his own. He felt himself growing hard in response to her moans coming from deep within her throat. Lightly biting her bottom lip and then licking it, Gregory looked at her flushed cheeks and rapid breathing.

"Size 6," Gregory said.

"What?" She was trying to compose herself.

"Your ring size, I'm guessing a 6," answered Gregory. Samantha couldn't believe that was what he was thinking about after a kiss like that.

"Yes, ready to go?" If only she knew how ready he was, thought Gregory.

"Sure," he answered. "Let's get you something to eat first so you don't pass out on me again. We have time before we meet the jewelers."

Chapter 6 Diamonds

Pulling up in front of a local jewelry store, Samantha looked at all of the quaint shops along the main street of town. She never shopped here before and just loved the feeling in this area.

"I'm all about supporting local businesses and these jewelers have some beautiful rings that I would love to show you. The owner is a college buddy of mine; he and his wife run this successful business," said Gregory. "They should be ready for us, shall we?"

With his hand extended to Samantha, she knew there was no turning back and walked into the store together.

"Gregory! We are so happy for you!" exclaimed Mary, who was the store owner. "And you must be Samantha!" Mary gave her a big welcoming hug. "David, get out here! Gregory is here!"

"Relax woman, I'm coming!" shouted David. Around the corner came a big, burly football type of a guy. "Well you ole devil you! You are taking the plunge!" David and Gregory gave each other a big brotherly hug. "And you must be Samantha. Wow! Where did you hide her Greg! It's so nice to meet you!" David gave Samantha a big bear hug too. Gregory stood back and watched this exchange between his future wife and his best friend from college.

"Sam, this is David, my best friend from college and his wife Mary. Figured we would come here as they have beautiful, unique jewelry and he would kill me if I didn't give him our business."

"Damned straight!" agreed David. "More importantly, to be a part of this celebration, that's the best news we've had all year!"

David already had rings put aside to show them. After an hour of looking at the rings, they both settled on a teardrop shaped diamond and sapphire engagement ring. It was very sweet, nothing over the top as Samantha wouldn't feel comfortable with that. It was very feminine, just like she is thought Gregory. He also picked up a pair of diamond stud earrings and a diamond heart shaped pendant to take with them for when they had an evening out with clients. Without Samantha knowing it, he had Mary wrap up a diamond tennis bracelet as a wedding present from him. Even though this was a contracted marriage, he wanted to get her something as a thank you for the sacrifices for the year ahead. He planned on spoiling her and often.

"It's time for a toast to the happy couple," exclaimed David. He popped open the champagne bottle while Mary poured four glasses. Gregory walked over to Samantha and put his arm around her. Finding herself relaxing against him, Gregory had said they had to make this look real to everyone but was finding out that it wasn't really hard to pretend. That very thought shocked her. She actually liked Gregory Steele, probably more than she should. Each holding a glass upwards, David toasted the happy couple.

"To my dear friend Gregory and his beautiful bride Samantha," David said. "May you have many years of happiness and love like Mary and I have. May you enjoy the excitement, joys and pleasure and hurdle over any sorrows that will only strengthen your love and commitment to each other. We couldn't be happier for the both of you! Congratulations!"

As the four of them drank their champagne, Samantha noticed how David just worshiped Mary. She could tell just by the way they were with each other and the love they shared, even with this toast. It was something that Samantha had wished for herself but that would have to wait a year or two for now.

"For you Samantha, will you do the honor of being my wife?" David handed Gregory the beautiful diamond and sapphire engagement ring.

"Yes Gregory, I will," smiled Samantha. She couldn't help but have tears in her eyes as he gently slipped the ring on her finger. She wasn't sure if the tears were from knowing this marriage was for only a year or because she started to have deeper feelings for him. That thought startled her even more. Gregory smiled down at her and lowered his lips to hers for a sweet endearing kiss that seemed to last forever but only lasted a brief moment. With his fingers, he wiped the tears from her cheeks as Samantha knew that she was in danger of losing her heart to this man. Holding her left hand in his, Gregory raised her hand and kissed it by the ring. He couldn't take his eyes off of hers. Giving her hand a little squeeze, he motioned that it was time to leave.

"We have to get going guys," Gregory said. "Thank you both for everything and look for the invite in the mail too." As they exited the store, they noticed it was already lunchtime and they were both hungry.

"How about lunch Sam? This town has so many nice places. We have time before we have to go to the lawyer."

"Sure, that sounds just lovely," agreed Samantha. She couldn't help but look at the ring on her left hand.

"Do you like it?" Gregory asked.

"I love it, thank you," said Samantha. Seeing the ring on her left hand made this all very real now. Samantha calmed her nerves by focusing her attention at the different stores until they slowed down. Pulling up in front of an Italian cafe, he came around to help her out of the car. It was a perfect place with a beautiful area to sit outside to enjoy the warmer weather.

"Would you mind if we sat outside Gregory?" Holding her hand, Gregory had the hostess seat them outside to enjoy their lunch.

"This is so lovely," commented Samantha while looking around her.

"So are you Sam," remarked Gregory. "Are you ok with all of this? I don't want you to be sad at all like you seemed at the store."

"No I'm fine. It's just that all girls dream of this day, getting the ring, planning their wedding, spending the rest of their life with the man of their dreams. I'm just missing a few steps here," explained Samantha.

"Well, let's just see where this all goes," said Gregory. At that moment, the waitress came over to get their orders. Deciding on a brick oven pizza with homemade mozzarella and basil on top was a unanimous decision. Sitting back drinking a beer, Gregory thought this would be a good time to get to know Samantha on a more personal level.

"So Sam, tell me about your family so I can get to know more about you."

"Ok it makes sense that you should know in case someone asks you about me. My parents died in a car accident when I was 10 years old. They were wonderful parents and had a strong marriage. They wouldn't understand this arrangement at all. I was their only child. My Aunt Elaine, my Father's sister, raised me. I adore her but she is one sharp lady. You will have to be one step ahead of her or forget it. Aunt Elaine never married so raising me was something she thought she would never experience in her life so we basically saved each other," smiled Samantha. Gregory didn't miss the shining quality in her eyes when she spoke about her family and Aunt.

"Where does she live?"

"Right here in Boston. I keep in touch with her all the time as she is in her late 70's now. I will have to bring you with me for a visit as she will expect to meet you when I tell her about you."

"Will you tell her about this deal we have made?"

"Yes, I will tell her the truth," Samantha said. "We have a very strong relationship, she may not love this but I won't lie to her about it. Trust me, she will definitely let us know how she feels about it," giggled Samantha. "It looks like our pizza is here!"

Glad for the reprieve of speaking about her family, Samantha dished out a slice for Gregory and then served herself.

"So now it's your turn. Tell me about your family."

"Ok. My parents are James and Diana. They live in Portland, Maine, near where my estate is. Dad is a retired attorney and Mom a retired school teacher. They met when they were in college and fell madly in love. A few years after they got married, they had my brother Michael. Two years later they had me. You will meet my brother shortly as he is the attorney that has drawn up the contract for us. He took over Dad's firm and expanded it. We both had what I guess would be a normal childhood. Good schooling, a loving home. Since mom didn't have a daughter, she made sure that we learned how to cook and do our own laundry so we would be good husband material. She believed that we were to be equal partners with our wives and be there to help them out. Because of her, I make a mean steak and roasted potatoes," smiled Gregory.

"I look forward to that," smiled Samantha.

"So do I," agreed Gregory. Taking a sip of beer, he continued with his story.

"Michael is still single, he was engaged but that fell apart two months before his wedding day. He's a workaholic, looks like a young Robert Redford, but please don't tell him that. It goes right to his head," laughed Greg. "He's my best friend, a great guy. Speaking of which, we need to get going. He's the punctual type."

Realizing what a relaxing lunch they just had, she saw a different side to Gregory. A good family life, it was something she missed out on. She was actually looking forward to meeting his family but a thought crossed her mind. Does his family know about this arrangement? Gregory took care of the bill, helped her into the car and they were on their way. As Gregory maneuvered the Maserati into traffic, Samantha asked him if his family knew their real story. "My brother obviously does but my parents don't. I don't think I will tell them the truth. Dad will start to find loopholes in everything and mom, well she wouldn't understand anything like this for business ventures. So right now, I won't tell them." Gregory pulled up in front of The Steele/Harris Law Firm building.

"Well, we're here," said Gregory. As he has done before, Gregory opened the car door for her and helped her out. He sensed her anxiety over this step of their agreement as he was feeling it too but for different reasons. He was already having serious feelings about her and he was trying hard not to.

"It will be fine Sam." He was trying to convince himself of this too. Taking her hand in his, he escorted her to the elevator as they started to the top floor. Samantha's heart was beating so hard in her chest as the elevator started upwards to the law firm. She kept looking at the numbers as they got closer to the law firm. Gregory started rubbing his thumb again in her palm to relax her. Turning her face up to his, he captured her lips in an all consuming kiss that made all thoughts of anxiety go out the window. Pushing her up against the elevator wall, Samantha felt all of him as his body moved close to her. His hand brushed up against her breast as his lips came down hard on hers. Holding her arms above her head, Samantha arched her body into his as Gregory's lips kissed the soft part of her neck by her ear. The sound of her moaning out loud made him bite into her shoulder. She pulled her arms down and held his face between her hands. Kissing him full on the lips, she rubbed herself on his thigh that was pressed up against her. Something inside of Gregory snapped as he couldn't get enough of this gorgeous woman. He gave of himself but demanded the same from her. She knew that if she ever invited him to share her bed, he would be a passionate lover. Samantha felt she could sign the papers now; that Gregory would take care of her this next year and she would reciprocate. Lifting his mouth from hers, he kissed the top of her nose and winked at her while looking down at her. He thinks he's so charming and in reality, he definitely was. Samantha could lose her heart to this man and started thinking of boundaries again.

"Is this part of the honeymoon plans you were telling me about last night?"

Without having time to answer, the elevator door opened while they still had their arms around each other. Since it was Saturday, there were only a handful of people in the office working on cases which made Samantha feel more at ease. As if sensing them, Michael turned and saw what was going on in the elevator. He didn't miss seeing the embrace his brother had around his future sister in law and saw how attracted his brother was to Samantha. This was going to be interesting year thought Michael. Meeting them halfway to his office, Michael gave his brother a hug and slap on the back. It was obvious this was a close family and a strong brother relationship. Looking at the two of them, Samantha thought what gorgeous looking men. One so dark and the other did look like a young Robert Redford. They must have attractive parents.

"So here is my future sister-in-law!" said Michael. He gave Samantha a big hug to welcome her into the family. Looping her arm thru his, Michael escorted Samantha to his office.

"So are you sure you want to marry my brother? I'm available," smiled Michael.

"Hey big brother," laughed Gregory. "She's mine."

"Technically, not yet," responded Michael. "Let's go to my office and go thru the terms of this agreement."

After seating Samantha in a chair, Gregory sat next to her as Michael took his seat behind his desk.

"Ok then, here's a copy for you Samantha and one for you Greg. It's pure and simple. A stipend of $20,000 per month for 12 months, the ring, jewelry, clothes, and rent paid for a year. Samantha will reside where you are Gregory, either at your apartment in Boston or at the estate in Portland with her own living quarters unless she decides differently. Samantha will still retain her position as VP of

Public Relations at the firm. At the end of the year's time, a divorce will be granted if you both still want that."

Michael sat back to look at the both of him. As an attorney, he had to ask this question.

"What will you both do if Samantha becomes pregnant?" Dead silence greeted that question. "I'm being serious Greg. Listen, I'm not blind. I can see there is an attraction between the both of you. I saw that when you both came off the elevator. A year is a long time to be together and not be together, if you know what I mean."

Turning a pretty shade of pink, Samantha decided to answer his question.

"If something happens, which I don't believe it will, I will take precautions," Samantha said.

"Thank you for bringing this up Mike. We would take the necessary precautions," Gregory said. Looking at each of them, Michael thought good luck. She's beautiful and my brother is very attracted to her. Michael wished he had someone to bet money with that they would end up together happily ever after. This was going to be a fun year watching the both of them.

"Ok then, let's get you on the road to marriage." Giving them each a pen, all the papers were signed.

"You are all set then. Congratulations. If you need anything Samantha, feel free to reach out to me. Here's my card," Michael said.

"Thank you so much," Samantha said.

"Thanks Mike," Gregory said.

"What are you going to tell Mom and Dad?"

"Not the truth, that's for sure. Dad will want to see the contract and Mom would be incredibly upset. Let's just keep this to the three of us," Gregory said.

"I'll plead the 5th amendment if they find out," laughed Michael.

"Thanks a lot Mike," Gregory said.

"I'll get everything all set with the Judge to officiate it. Just let me know what day."

"That's great Mike, thanks."

As Samantha and Gregory walked down the hall, he reached for her hand and squeezed it. "Thank you Sam. No other words but thank you." Both were in their own thoughts as they rode down the elevator. Once in the car, he turned to her to discuss their wedding date. He was trying not to sound so stilted and business like but it just came out that way.

"We'll get married by Justice of the Peace. Mike will be my Best Man and I'm guessing Ronni will be your Maid of Honor. Would you want your Aunt to attend?"

"I'm sure Aunt Elaine will want to attend," Samantha said.

"We should get this done as soon as possible," Gregory said. "I will give you the day off for this event." Samantha caught herself smiling as she caught his sly smile and began to relax a bit. Gregory seemed to have a way of calming her down with his sense of humor. "I would hope you would give me the day off. I guess I should pack what I will need and bring things to your place?"

"I'll help you and organize movers too but let's relax for the rest of the day. I want to take you to my apartment so you can see where you will be living. I think you will love it."

"Ok," agreed Samantha. She thought it would calm her nerves a bit if she saw where she was going to be living for the next year. Moving back into traffic, both Gregory and Samantha kept their thoughts to themselves. Gregory turned on the radio to one of the rock stations so he didn't have to engage into a conversation with Samantha. He needed this time to think things thru about their upcoming marriage. Things were starting to get a little complicated with his feelings towards her as this was fast becoming less of a business relationship for him anyway. Not knowing how Samantha felt, he decided he would take the necessary steps to get to know her and see if this could be something more. Samantha saw that they were getting off at the exit near the water. The condos in this area were beautiful. Of course Gregory would live in this exclusive area. Pulling into the complex, Gregory parked his car in his assigned place. They entered the gorgeous apartment building that overlooked the bay.

"Good afternoon Mr. Steele," the doorman said.

Introducing Samantha as his fiancée, Gregory picked up his mail and the dry cleaning that was left for him as they took the next elevator up to the 12th floor. Not quite the penthouse but it could have been, Gregory opened the door and the view was breathtaking. A wall of windows which overlooked the bay gave her a magnificent view that no painting could compete with. In the living room were a soft, plush leather sofa and two love seats in a rich cocoa brown. She also noticed a leather recliner near the flat screen TV where she figured was Gregory's domain to unwind at the end of the day. In the other corner was a desk setup with a flat screen computer and a phone so he could conduct business at home when needed. With its open layout, she saw a view of beautiful granite and steel appliance kitchen and a quaint breakfast area. Beyond that was a formal dining room. It was quite beautiful and very comfortable.

"So this is the main area," Gregory said. "Let me show you the rest of the apartment."

Walking down the hall, he stopped at the first bedroom. "This is my room and bathroom. It also has that gorgeous view." Putting away his dry cleaning, he watched Samantha as she looked at everything. He had dark wooden furniture in his bedroom with a hunter green comforter set on a king sized bed. His bathroom was modern with a huge marble step down bathtub. Her mind started drifting to where it shouldn't have been and Gregory sensed that.

"Let me show you where you will be."

He opened the door to a beautifully decorated room, pastel colors, a plush carpet and the same beautiful scene outside a wall of windows.

"I figured you would want to bring your own bed and furnishings so I just had them paint and put in the carpet. Thru this door is your bathroom."

It was a dream; a marble counter top, matching marble bathtub and a huge walk in closet that you could easily make into a small sitting room if you wanted to. Gregory caught Samantha smiling at that.

"I'm guessing that this is every woman's dream," smiled Gregory.

"This is all very beautiful Gregory," said Samantha while trying to stifle a yawn. Gregory saw her yawning and the dark circles under her eyes.

"Listen, today has been an exhausting one," Gregory said. "Why don't you go lie down and take a nap. I have some business things to take care of now. I'm planning on making us dinner before I take you home. Sound good?"

"Yes sir," Samantha said. She went into Gregory's bedroom, took off her shoes and was asleep the minute her head touched his pillow.

Chapter 7 First Dinner

An hour later, Gregory peered into the bedroom. Seeing that Samantha was still fast asleep, Gregory realized he was exhausted too so he joined her. Lying on his side, he gathered Samantha against him. It wasn't lost on him about how perfectly they fit together. Catching the scent of her hair and feeling her curves against his body, he knew he had to get some control over his emotions with her. His last thought before he fell asleep was to give Paul an extra bonus for picking out the right woman for this job.

As Samantha started waking up, she felt Gregory's arm lying casually across her breasts and his strong thigh across her leg. She could feel Gregory's arousal and didn't want to move for fear of waking him. He had looked as tired as she did and wanted him to rest too. This agreement was a stressful change for the both of them, but in her case, Samantha was starting to have strong feelings for Gregory. She didn't know if it would ever be reciprocated and that thought made her a bit sad. For now, she would take each day as it came. Knowing that she would be with Gregory was what she would have to settle with for the time being. Looking at the beautiful sunset outside her window, Samantha didn't know that Gregory was awake and was enjoying just holding her.

"I never get tired of this view, especially at this time of day," whispered Gregory so as not to startle her. Rolling to his side, Gregory pulled Samantha towards him.

"What do you say that I fix us some spaghetti and put you on salad duty?" Samantha pulled herself up with her chin resting on his chest. He tried so hard to keep his mind off her breasts being crushed on his chest but was failing miserably. She didn't realize the effect she was having on him.

"Sure, I can do that," Samantha said. She sat up a little further and he could see her nipples showing thru her tee-shirt. He also noticed the scratches on her neck.

"What's this from?" Gregory was curious as he touched her throat.

"I had a dream the other night and I must have pulled off my cross as it was on the floor and I was left with these scratches." explained Samantha.

"That must have been some dream," Gregory said.

"You were in it," said Samantha. She felt a little daring tempting him with this story. Ronni would be proud of her. A look of realization came over Gregory.

"So that's what you meant when you said it's you after you almost fainted. Now how did I become a part of your dream?"

"I'm reading Carlotta's new manuscript. The leading man in the story looks like you," Samantha said. "People at the office told her you were very handsome so she Googled you. You instantly became her leading man and showed up in my dream."

"And what was I doing to you in your dream?"

"You said you have been watching and waiting for this moment and that I had to come to you willingly. Then you were biting my neck." giggled Samantha.

"That must have been some dream, let's make it a reality."

Without warning, Gregory pulled Samantha down under him as his hands moved up over her breasts. He put his leg between the both of hers so as to get them as close to each other as they could while wearing clothes. There was no mistaking the desire he felt for her. He claimed her mouth in a kiss that shook her to her very core. Pulling him closer to her, he released her mouth as he traveled down to her neck and to her breasts. Lightly biting her nipples thru her tee-shirt and bra, Samantha was just about ready to throw in the towel until her cell phone starting ringing. Moaning that she should get it, Gregory moved back to her mouth, coaxing her attention back to him.

It started ringing again and Samantha pushed him up from her. With a devilish smile, Gregory lay back on his pillows and watched her grab for the phone.

A breathless Samantha answered the phone on the sixth ring.

"Well hello there Sam," chuckled Ronni. "Please tell me you are in bed with that gorgeous soon to be husband of yours."

"Yes but not like you think," answered Samantha.

"Ok I'm guessing he is there right now so I won't keep you. Just wanted to see if we are still on for tomorrow?"

"Yes for sure. We have shopping to do tomorrow. So see you in the morning," Samantha said.

"I'll be there and I want to hear stories from you too. Have a good night," replied Ronni. Samantha replied the same to her and hung up.

"She's a good friend to you," stated Gregory.

"The best," replied Samantha. "Ok chef, get out of bed and let's get dinner ready. I want to see how good you really are."

Gregory lunged for her but Samantha managed to get out of his reach quickly and ran to the kitchen. Together they enjoyed preparing dinner with each other. Gregory made Samantha sample his sauce recipe and Samantha fed him fresh mozzarella and tomatoes. She set the table while he opened up a bottle of wine. Pouring her a glass and then himself, he raised his glass for a toast.

"Let's toast to us and this venture; to our journey. And thank you Sam."

"You are very welcome. I'm here to help you get this job done and I promise to do it well." Sitting down, they enjoyed their first home made dinner, the first of what would be many.

"Is there anything that you need or something that I missed in this planning?"

"Nothing that I can think of," Samantha answered. "I'll get my shopping done tomorrow with Ronni and just have to pack what I need."

Finishing up dinner, they cleaned up together and then it was time for Gregory to drive her home. It was quiet in the car as each of them was in their own thoughts about their upcoming wedding. Pulling up in front of her apartment, he put the car in park.

Reaching over to Samantha, Gregory grabbed her shoulders and pulled her towards him. He needed to know that their attraction was real. Looking down at her, he kissed her with such passion that Samantha couldn't help herself but sigh in his arms. Samantha's response was exactly what he needed. Trailing his lips down her neck, Samantha grabbed hold of his shoulders with her nails digging into him thru his shirt. Gregory was the first to start to pull away from Samantha as they had to calm down before things went out of control. Reaching into his wallet, he took out his credit card.

"Here you go Sam. Spare no expense. You know what you need to buy for entertaining." She started laughing as it seemed so funny to be given his credit card after the kiss they just shared.

"I know what you are thinking Sam but trust me. You will be my wife and will be taken care of as such," Gregory said. Giving her a quick kiss on the lips, Samantha let herself out of the car.

As Gregory drove away, she looked at her left hand. The diamond sparkled back at her making this very real. She would do her best to hold up her end of the bargain and enjoy the time they have together for the next year. Not wanting to think any more about it, she let herself into her apartment and surprisingly, got a good night's sleep.

Chapter 8 Shopping Spree Part Two

Waking up early, Samantha was feeling refreshed and happy as she turned on the Sunday morning news. She had an hour before Ronni picked her up so she thought now was better than ever to call her Aunt Elaine. She was already going to see her at 3 o'clock but wanted to tell her that Ronni would be there too.

Punching in her number, a boisterous Aunt Elaine answered on the third ring.

"Hello Sam. It's wonderful having caller ID. I know who is calling me before I answer. Are you still coming to visit me this afternoon?"

"Yes of course. I just wanted to let you know that I'll be bringing Ronni with me too for a visit," Samantha said.

"I really like that girl. Reminds me of me at her age, wild and free," chuckled Aunt Elaine. "Is everything ok Samantha? I have a feeling that something is wrong."

"No Auntie. Everything is just fine. I just wanted you to know that we will both be there later."

"Ok Sam. Have fun and I'll see the both of you later."

Samantha hung up the phone with a smile on her face. She loved her Aunt very much and wondered how she was going to take the news of her upcoming wedding. Then she thought of Gregory and how sexy he was to her. She imagined being taken by him, heart, body and mind. She didn't know how long she could fight these feelings of wanting him. After a few days of knowing him, Samantha knew she wanted him more than anyone she has ever known. The kind of man he was, he would demand nothing but her whole being and would give her the same.

Until that inevitable day comes, she had to keep the flame of desire in check or try as best as she could. Even though this was a "job" she was hired for, Samantha knew she was in danger of losing herself to him. Ronni let herself into Samantha's apartment as she didn't respond to her knocking on the door. She just looked at Samantha staring off into space and started snapping her fingers in front of her.

"Oh soon to be Mrs. or Ms. Steele, let me see you. You look like a woman with a man on her mind," said Ronni. "He's a hot one at that. Look at that ring. Wow Sam! This is really happening!"

"He's amazing Ronni. I'm in serious danger of falling for him and I don't know how long before I give into my feelings," sighed Samantha.

"Listen Sam, I can tell you are starting to really like him, maybe even love him. Just take one day at a time. Get to know him. But I have to say, there is a current between the both of you," Ronni said. "That day when you almost fainted and I ran into your office, I had to leave because I felt something electric between the both of you. I felt like I intruded in on something. He's the type of man that knows what he wants and he wants you. And when that happens, you will be one well loved woman. Come on, let's get out there and do some shopping. You need a whole new wardrobe!"

"Thank you Ronni. What would I do without you?" Checking to see that she had Gregory's credit card, she locked her apartment door and off they went.

Heading downtown, both girls ended up at their favorite boutique. Samantha bought several cocktail dresses, one little black dress, and another cocktail dress in a deep cranberry color and a gorgeous white suit to add to her wardrobe. She also chose a full length black form fitting evening gown, with sleeves that came off the shoulder and dipped a little lower in the front which showed off her beautiful neckline. She would wear this dress for their party in a few weeks. Shoes, evening bags completed that part of the wardrobe.

"Sam, you have to get this!" Ronni turned around holding a vintage gown, form fitted with beautiful bead work and a little train. It was a rich cream color, perfect for her wedding.

"That is stunning Ronni!" Samantha said. "That's my wedding dress!" She went over to take a closer look and fell in love with it. Luckily, it was in her size. So that dress was gently wrapped to add to her purchases. A few more suits and casual dresses completed her shopping spree. She was very happy with the garments and thought Gregory would be very happy.

"Oh Sam, you forgot a few more things, don't forget your trousseau," teased Ronni.

"Really Ronni?"

Smiling at Samantha, Ronni brought out the lingerie sets. Samantha settled on a sexy black thing that left nothing to the imagination, a pink teddy with a robe, a white lace shift and a cream man's style loungewear silk pajama set.

"Well, you know Sam, you don't need many things as I don't think you will be wearing them very long," laughed Ronni.

The image of Gregory on top of her was almost too much to think about. Just at that moment, her cell phone rang and it was him.

"How's the shopping spree going?"

"Very well, you will be pleased. Ronni's been a great help too," said Samantha

"We're in the lingerie department," shouted Ronni.

"Knock it off Ronni," laughed Samantha.

Hearing Gregory laugh, he started getting a visual of Samantha in different lingerie sets, her sexy body covered in lace and maybe not that much lace. They definitely wouldn't stay on long if he had his way with her.

"Well I'm glad you are having a good time shopping." Stopping for a second, Gregory wondered if he should tell her what he was feeling at that moment. Oh what the Hell. No one is going to revoke my man card. "I missed seeing you today, and holding you," admitted Gregory. "I don't know why I just told you that, I'm sorry if I was out of line." Against her better judgment, she felt the same.

"I missed kissing you today," admitted Samantha. Hearing his sharp intake of breath, Gregory closed his eyes on the other end of the phone. This agreement wasn't supposed to be like this. He has never wanted a woman like he wanted Samantha.

"Well, I'll have to remedy that when I see you." Gregory said. "See you later."

Samantha hung up with Ronni looking at her.

"Wow, stick a fork in you, you are so done," laughed Ronni. "Let's go, don't want to keep Aunt Elaine waiting." After paying the very large bill, they loaded up her car and headed to Aunt Elaine's home.

Chapter 9 Aunt Elaine

Aunt Elaine was the dearest person in Samantha's life. She raised Samantha when her parents were both killed in a car accident. Taking in a young Samantha while running her own advertising agency created challenges for Aunt Elaine, but it was one job that she had gladly taken on. Samantha meant the world to her and together they survived the loss of Samantha's parents. As the girls drove up to her house, Aunt Elaine was sitting on the porch waiting for them.

"Samantha!" exclaimed Aunt Elaine. "You are glowing. Ronni, how beautiful you look. Come on in girls so we can catch up!"

Aunt Elaine's home was very cozy, early American. One felt very welcome when you went there.

"I have lunch set up on the patio. Then you can explain to me what that ring is on Sam's left hand."

Walking behind Aunt Elaine, Ronni whispered under her breath.

"That woman doesn't miss a trick, does she?"

"I heard that!" exclaimed Aunt Elaine.

Sitting down, Samantha started to explain everything to her Aunt, right down to the contract and the shopping spree.

"So he is paying me a generous salary per month, paying my rent, clothes, basically anything I need and I have to stay with him at his residences, can't date anyone for a year as we will be married in name only," explained Samantha

"What's his name again? I believe something Steele. I remember reading something about him in my Celebrity Insider Magazine about 6 months ago. Ronni, look him up on that phone of yours."

"His name is Gregory Auntie," said Samantha.

"Has he been treating you well? Are you falling in love with him?"

Before Samantha could answer, Ronni shouted out, "Bingo! Here it is. CEO millionaire Gregory Steele of Crescendo Steele Publishing splits with girlfriend and socialite Alexandra Whitley. An alleged affair between Ms. Whitley and one of Mr. Steele's senior managers has resulted in the manager being fired and Ms. Whitley out of his stable."

Putting down her cell phone, Ronni had it all figured out. "So this makes total sense. The foreign businessmen think Gregory is a playboy so he needs a wife to solve his problem and in comes Sam," Ronni said.

"Are you falling in love with him?" Her Aunt was staring intently at Samantha.

Ronni was shaking her head in a resounding yes and Samantha had tears in her eyes.

"I'm trying hard not to," admitted Samantha.

"I'm familiar with affairs of the heart Sam. Just because I didn't marry doesn't mean I didn't have my share of lovers. I understand what you are going thru. I want to meet this young man. When is the wedding?"

"Thursday, Justice of the Peace," Samantha said.

"Ok, I will be there Samantha. You are as close to a daughter that I've ever had. I hope that this "job" ends up with a happy ending too. It wouldn't be the choice I would want for you but there are feelings there for him. I can see that. Bring him by after work this week so I can meet him. I'll make sure to have dinner ready so we can enjoy our evening."

"Ok Auntie, I will," Samantha said. "He has been very generous and very respectful too; I want you to know that."

"He's drop dead gorgeous," added Ronni.

"Ronni, you aren't helping here," Samantha said. She couldn't help but laugh at Ronni, she always had something to say to break the tension in any given situation.

"Well, I look forward to meeting your Gregory Samantha. I want to see for myself what this situation is all about. I promise not to embarrass him, well not too much anyway," Aunt Elaine said. "Now let's enjoy our lunch and have some more girl talk."

As always, they both enjoyed Aunt Elaine's witty company. Sharp as can be and very forth coming, she was just wonderful to be around. She was very good at challenging them to excel in their line of work and also with relationships, kind of a self appointed life coach. They always enjoyed their visits with her. Finishing their lunch, they said their goodbyes with Samantha promising to bring Gregory by to meet her early in the week.

Ronni dropped Sam off at her apartment with all of her purchases. Not going up with Sam as she wanted to get home, Ronni thanked her for a fun day. With a promise of seeing her at the office in the morning, Ronni drove off.

Chapter 10 Temptation

Laying out all of her new clothes in the living room, Samantha poured herself a glass of wine and looked over everything. Blushing as she held up the black lingerie that left nothing to the imagination, she heard the doorbell ring. She couldn't believe that Ronni talked her into getting this item that really didn't cover a thing.

"Who is it?"

"You're soon to be husband," Gregory answered.

Feeling excitement start to build, Samantha pressed the intercom. "I just got home. Come on up." She opened the door a crack and quickly went into the bathroom to make sure she looked presentable. Coming back in to the living room, Gregory was looking at the lingerie sets that were on the couch. Samantha was embarrassed to see that he was holding up the black one.

"Well, hello there Ms. Hartley. What do we have here?" Gregory put the lingerie down and came over to her.

"Just a little something for the honeymoon," Samantha said.

"I would say that is a little something. I'm looking forward to seeing you in it, if I'm allowed that is," Gregory answered. "But for now, I have something for you."

In his other hand, he carried a small bouquet of flowers. In her best southern accent, Samantha couldn't help but tease him.

"I do declare Sir; I swear that you are courting me!" Putting the flowers down on the table, Gregory bowed in front of her.

"Yes Ma'am, I am but I think this way is much more effective." He pulled Samantha close to him. "I want to know you."

Samantha looked deep into his eyes. Touching his face, she offered her mouth to his. With a groan, Gregory took control of the situation, his tongue relentless, teasing her. His hand caressed her breast as it started making its way to the juncture between her legs. Samantha knew they were getting to the point of no return but she wanted him.

"I need you Sam, like no other."

As she looked at him, Samantha extended her hand to him and gave him a seductive smile. He took her hand and in one move, picked her up and headed to the bedroom. Once there, he put her down on the floor and started kissing her again.

"Are you sure?"

"Yes, please. I need you Gregory." And those were all the words he needed. Pulling off her tee-shirt, he buried his face between her breasts. They had a life of their own with the attention he was paying to them. She could hardly stand so she leaned up against him. Raising her arms up, she pulled his shirt off and sucked in her breath at the beauty of him. His muscular chest had a scattering of dark hair on it; his strong arms drove her insane with wanting him. He let her explore him with her hands. As she brought her hand down to his belt, Samantha slowly undid it to get some control over her emotions. He started unbuttoning her jeans as she unbuttoned his.

"God you are gorgeous Sam."

Gregory pulled her jeans off of her. Laying her on the bed, he undid the rest of his jeans and there was no mistaking that Gregory desired her. Lying on the bed next to her, he started to explore her with his mouth. His hands undid her bra and released her breasts to his touch. Writhing on her bed, he continued downwards between her legs. Lowering her panties, he teased her with his mouth until she cried out that she needed him. He continued licking and sucking her as she begged him for more. Putting his finger inside of her, she arched her back off the bed as she surrendered to his loving attack on her body. Before she had a chance to quiet down, Gregory came back up to her mouth, kissing her so that she tasted herself on him. Digging her nails into his chest, she felt the tip of his penis slowly enter her as she moaned in pleasure at the feelings he was causing. Red hot heat seared thru the both of them as he entered her as far as he could go. Samantha moved her hips under him while Gregory just stopped for a moment.

"Please Sam, give me a second. I don't want to come fast like a kid in high school. But if this is quick, I will make it up to you love, we have all night. You feel beyond amazing." Samantha gave him a slight smile and pulled his face to hers for a passionate kiss. Gregory started moving within her. She matched his rhythm, soaring higher and higher with him. Wrapping her legs around his hips, he felt her tighten around him in a vice like grip that made him feel better than good. He knew she was almost there as Samantha cried out his name in pleasure and Gregory followed her down the abyss, crying out his pleasure too. This woman has made him feel like no one has as though she were made just for him. Gregory knew he shared something special with her. They both hugged and kissed each other as Samantha had tears in her eyes from the beauty of it.

"Hey," said Gregory looking down upon her. Samantha touched his face, along his jaw line.

"I don't know what happened here but it was beautiful," Samantha said.

"You are beautiful," remarked Gregory. He rolled to his back and took Samantha with him. Deep in thought, he knew at this moment, this just wasn't a woman for a job but a partner for life. He needed to work thru his feelings as he didn't want any attachment but that was before he met Samantha.

"Are you ok?" She was studying the range of emotions crossing his face and hoped he wasn't regretting what just happened. Turning his head towards hers, Gregory gave her that smile that she was already in love with.

"You surprise me at every turn and I love it," Gregory said. Noticing his tattoo on his upper arm, Samantha reached over to trace it with her finger.

"This design is beautiful. Does it mean anything?"

"It means courage and boldness. I had it done when I was completing my Masters. Dave and I were both in the Business Administration program and knew we would go into our own businesses after graduation. So we went ahead and got tattoos to remind us to be warriors in business. Actually I think we were both drunk the night we got them. At least they were something that we could live with when we sobered up."

Moving her hand down his body, she explored the muscles that made up his stomach until her hand wrapped around his penis. Gregory just stared at Samantha. With her hair thoroughly tossed and sexy and her pouty lips red from a thorough loving, he watched her explore his body. God was she gorgeous.

"Well, I'm going to take a shower, care to join me?"

She moved her hand slowly up and down the length of him. That was his undoing.

"Yes Ma'am. Lead the way."

As the water got warm, Samantha coaxed him into the shower. It was her turn to pleasure him first. Letting the water cascade down their bodies, her mouth trailed down his neck and then to his chest. Her hand lightly grazed his nipple as her hands kept exploring his stomach down towards his erection that was waiting for her. Kissing him on the top part of his penis, she drove him wild with her mouth and hands. Licking and sucking him into her mouth, Gregory enjoyed how wet and warm her mouth felt on his dick. Holding onto the shower wall, he had his head thrown backwards, just enjoying the sensations that Samantha was causing. Looking back down at her was an erotic sight for him. Feeling that he was watching her, Samantha looked up at him. Not breaking eye contact with each other, she moaned deep in her throat at the intensity of feelings between the both of them. Samantha took Gregory into the back of her throat and then back out again.

"That's enough Sam. I need you to feel me deep inside of you so you have no doubt you are mine. I need you too much." Pulling her up to him, he picked her up and slammed into her as her back was up against the tile wall. This time was all and out passion, wanting to make her his forever and not just a year. Moving with an almost desperation inside her, Samantha wrapped her legs around his waist to bring her as close as she could to him.

"Please, faster Gregory," cried Samantha.

His mouth lightly biting her breasts, Gregory felt Samantha tighten around him as she climaxed. Crying out his name as her orgasm hit her hard, that was too much for Gregory to bear as he joined her in blissful satisfaction. Putting his head against hers, Gregory came to terms that this woman was working her way into his heart. He slowly lowered her to the ground and leaned into her with deep kisses as the water fell all around them. Grabbing the body wash, he poured it on them and massaged her between her legs, bringing her to wanton abandonment once again. Just as Samantha thought, Gregory was a demanding and giving lover. Samantha knew at this point that she loved him. There was no turning back. When she says her vows to him this week, in her heart she knew they would be for life and that she would always love him no matter what happened.

Gregory thru his head back to rinse the soap off and looked back down at her with that boyish smile that melted her heart.

"All good?"

"More than good," answered Samantha.

Shutting off the water, they toweled themselves off. Wrapping his arms around her, Gregory held her close against him.

"I'd like to stay if I may," Gregory said.

"I would like that but I can't be late for work tomorrow. Don't want to get the boss mad at me," teased Samantha.

"Oh I think you will have a good reason to be late for work. Besides, I have an "in" with him so don't worry about it," Gregory said.

It was well after midnight when they climbed back into bed. Setting the alarm for 7am, Samantha settled in Gregory's arms and fell to sleep. Gregory's last thought was that they didn't use protection and smiled at that thought.

Chapter 11 The Morning After

The beeping of her alarm woke Samantha out of a blissful slumber. Leaning over to her night stand, she hit it off and felt herself being drawn backwards into Gregory's rock hard chest. He wrapped both arms under her breasts and put his face into the back of her neck.

"Stay here for a few moments," Gregory whispered.

Samantha thought she had some time to spare before getting ready so she snuggled in closer and felt her eyes close again. It felt so good to have him in her bed, just feeling that they were the only two in the world at that moment. A few minutes went by when she felt his hands reach up to her nipples and start to caress them. He started kissing the back of her neck. One hand started it's downwards exploration and touched the inner core of her body. Samantha felt helpless to his touch as she moved in rhythm to what his fingers were doing to her. He moved them faster, bringing her to an early morning climax. Catching her breath, Samantha pushed Gregory on his back as she straddled him in one swift movement. She loved watching the emotions cross his face as she gave of herself freely with no restraint. She wanted to give him the same pleasure he had given to her. Moving her hips seductively, she controlled this part of their lovemaking and was driving him absolutely crazy with need. Throwing her head back with her hair cascading down her back, she was enjoying taking charge in giving Gregory pleasure. She leaned forward to kiss him passionately as she kept up the seductive pace she set for the both of them. Sitting up quickly, he held on to her. Then Samantha found herself on her back with Gregory looking down at her. Moving her leg farther apart, he was able to go deeper into her.

"Now who is teasing who?" said Gregory. He started moving slowly in and out of her.

"Please Gregory, don't make me wait."

That was all the invitation he needed. Moving his hips faster into hers, he brought both of them together, waves of emotion crashing over them until their passion slowed down with even breaths.

Gregory raised himself on his elbow while his hand pushed a stand of hair from her face. Slowly pulling himself out of her, he lovingly kissed this special lady that was stealing his heart.

"Good morning Sam," smiled Gregory. He rested his forehead on hers.

"Yes it is a good morning," agreed Samantha. "Look at the time. 8 o'clock. I'll grab a shower first. You stay here or I'll never get to work on time."

"I have a conference call meeting at 9:30 and then the doctor will be at the office to do our blood tests," Gregory said. Samantha jumped out of bed and blew him a kiss before she disappeared into the bathroom.

"There's coffee, cereal and bananas if you want. Help yourself!"

As Samantha stood under the shower, her blood ran cold. We didn't use any protection. It wasn't something she thought of in her moments of passion. It was obvious he didn't think about it either. She tried to remember when her cycle was but she couldn't think straight about it now. She needed to look at a calendar to calculate the time of month.

Turning off the shower, she smelled coffee brewing and smiled about how handy he was in the kitchen. Making a mental note to thank his mom when she met her, Samantha quickly toweled herself off. Her body felt tender in places from his loving touch. Catching herself in the mirror, she looked different somehow. Maybe more womanly after discovering how Gregory made her feel and how she satisfied him too. Let's hope I'm not pregnant now. Holding that thought, she brushed her teeth, dried her hair, and added light makeup.

Running to her closet, she put on cream colored sleeveless dress that had a matching jacket and navy and cream sling backs.

Walking into the kitchen, Gregory let out a long wolf whistle. Smiling at him, she grabbed a mug and made her usual green tea. He ran into the bathroom to take a quick shower too and came out 15 minutes later, dressed and toweling his hair. Looking amazingly sexy with fresh stubble on his face, she felt weak in the knees seeing him. Smiling at her from across the room, he was just about ready to leave for his apartment. To Hell with the boundaries she kept thinking about. They already crossed the line and she wasn't sorry for one minute.

"Don't worry about the towel Gregory. I'll put it in the hamper before I leave."

She put her mug in the sink and washed her hands. Gregory came up behind her to give her a hug and kiss her on her neck.

"Oh, I've told Aunt Elaine about us," Samantha said.

"Yes, ok," Gregory said. He turned Samantha around to face him. He kept kissing her neck.

"And she would love to meet you before our wedding day,"

Samantha continued. She was finding it very hard to concentrate now.

"Ok," Gregory said. He was still focused on her neck.

"Stop it," Samantha said laughing. "You are incorrigible."

"You drive me crazy with wanting you, do you realize that?" Samantha looked deep into his eyes and felt the same way about him.

"We should take things slowly, don't you think?" Samantha tried to move away from him but it was a losing battle. Gregory didn't say a word but gently took her jacket off of her. He slowly unzipped her dress while looking at her. As her dress slipped down her body, she stood before him in a lacey push up Demi bra with a matching thong that left nothing to the imagination. Stepping forward to Gregory, she slipped his shirt over his head and reached for his jeans. Slowly unzipping them, she eased them down over his hips, his erection clearly visible against his briefs. Picking her up so her legs straddled him, he laid her on top of her kitchen island and pulled her thong slowly down her legs. Moving his hands up her thighs, his fingers found what he was searching for and slowly moved them in and out of her, making her wild with need. Releasing his erection, he slowly eased himself deep within her. One hand at her breast and the other massaging her, Gregory was moving so slow, feeling every loving inch of her. Realizing she was close to the edge as he was, he picked up the pace which sent waves of passion crashing upon her. Gregory was joining her at the same time, enjoying his own pleasure deep inside her. He helped ease her to the floor while kissing her. Lifting his head, he looked at her. "How's that for slowing down?" She playfully hit him in response.

Gathering her dress and shoes, she ran back to the bathroom to take another shower. She had to get to the office. Getting redressed, she saw Gregory waiting for her. Touching her face, he gave her a kiss on her lips.

 "I will see you at the office after I shower and change at home. I had a beautiful time here with you last night and today."

"I did too Gregory, a beautiful time," Samantha said. Leaving her apartment hand in hand, he walked her to her car and kissed her.

"I'll see you later," Samantha said. "Oh I am so late. Bye."

Chapter 12 Surprise

Running into the building, the elevator was starting to close.

"Hold it please," Samantha shouted. Paul held open the door for her while she turned a lovely shade of pink.

"Hello Ms. Hartley, running a bit late today? Funny, Mr. Steele just called me saying he was running a little behind but had to go home first to get ready for work."

"Ok Paul, you know where he has been and thank you." Reaching up to him, she placed a kiss on his cheek.

"Very good Ms. Hartley. Glad to have been a part of this match making. I guess this match is a good one?"

Samantha just smiled in return. The elevator door opened and Samantha made a move to the conference room.

"Ms. Hartley, should I have green tea sent to the conference room for you? It doesn't look like you had enough time to pick your tea up."

"That would be amazing. You are an angel," Samantha said.

"So I'm told, "smiled Paul.

Samantha walked into the conference room to a group of people yelling congratulations. Ronni stepped forward and hugged her.

"Aren't you a little late this morning," Ronni whispered. Samantha felt the heat climb into her face. There were gifts on the table and a celebratory cake in the corner.

"I can't believe everything. This is quite a surprise!" Samantha said.

"Congratulations Ms. Hartley. We had no idea about you and Mr. Steele! Ronni said that she knew about you and Mr. Steele but was sworn to secrecy," said their accounts manager. Samantha spent the next half hour opening presents, hugging her co-workers and thanking them for their gifts and well wishes.

As short while later, Gregory walked into the room. A shout of congratulations came from the group again. Ronni went over to hug him.

"Congratulations Mr. Steele".

"Please call me Gregory," he whispered back to her. Ronni nodded as Gregory held onto Samantha's hand, smiling at his staff. They all took turns congratulating Gregory too. After twenty minutes of talking to everyone, Gregory came over to Samantha to let her know that the doctor was there to give them the blood tests and paperwork for their marriage. Hearing his name being called by his sales reps, Gregory went over to his staff to accept their congratulations. Samantha couldn't take her eyes off of him as he walked away from her.

"Well Sam, you look like you are undressing him with your eyes," laughed Ronni. Samantha turned a nice shade of pink while she looked at Ronni.

"I can't help myself," giggled Samantha. "Ronni, I have to get my blood test done so can you start and take over this meeting for a bit?"

"Sure, I can start with my part of the meeting and you can finish up." Looking at Samantha, she noticed the happiness that reached her eyes.

"So how was he?"Ronni asked impishly.

Samantha wasn't one to kiss and tell. She just gave Ronni a bright smile. Gregory watched these close friends smile at each other from across the room and knew he was the topic of their conversation. Thanking his sales reps, he walked back over to get Samantha for their appointment. He also thought of his brother Michael and maybe Ronni? This might be something to work on. Mike could use his life being turned upside down too and Ronni would be the just the woman to do that job.

"Sorry Ronni, I have to steal my fiancée for a bit."

"No problem, see you later Sam. Wanting to hold his hand but wanted to keep proper protocol in the office, Samantha and Gregory walked down to his office. As they past several of the employees, words of congratulations echoed thru the rooms. Reaching Gregory's office, Paul smiled proudly as not only were they are striking couple but he felt good in his heart that they belonged together.

"That should do it Ms. Hartley," said the doctor as he finished taking her blood sample.

"Here is your paperwork you both need Mr. Steele and also what you need to sign. Please make sure you bring this marriage certificate with you on Thursday."

"Thank you, we will," answered Gregory. Samantha and Gregory stood side by side as they signed the Marriage Certificate.

"Congratulations to you both," said the doctor. Gregory walked the doctor to the door and said goodbye to him. Samantha needed to get back to her meeting so she tried to follow the doctor out the door.

"Not so fast Ms. Hartley. You know by the State of Massachusetts,

we are already husband and wife. We just have to go thru the
formality."

"Oh really," said Samantha. As she put her arms around his neck,
Gregory lowered his mouth to hers and gently explored it. She let
out a little sigh and he smiled behind his kiss. Samantha traced her
fingers along the deep dimple of his smile. Catching her hand, he
kissed her palm as his eyes never left hers. It was just a special
moment between the two of them.

"So we can see your Aunt Elaine tonight. The next few nights will be
busy with moving and planning things," Gregory said.

"Great idea. I'll call her on my way back to the meeting," Samantha
said. "I really have to go." Gregory watched the sexy sway of her hips
as she headed back to the conference room.

"Paul, can you come in to start the list for the reception party for the
end of the month. It will be an event to introduce my wife to our
clients."

"Yes Mr. Steele. I've already put a tentative list together for you to
approve. It will be invitation only." And for the rest of the
afternoon, both Samantha and Gregory had full schedules and were
putting their own plans in place. The reception that is being planned
would be a Black Tie event at the exclusive Font de Riviera
Restaurant in downtown Boston. With 80 guests on the list, this was
a very important event.

"I think we have everyone covered Mr. Steele, including your brother and Aunt Elaine and their guests. I've also contacted the local newspapers to announce your upcoming marriage this week which will also go out to the national and international business magazines and publishers updates."

"Thank you. Please see to the invitations immediately. It will be hors devours and an open bar. I would love the venue for 4 hours and a band. Just enough time to talk some business, introduce Samantha and just enjoy ourselves," Gregory said. "Make sure we have the patio and Cubans for whoever wants to smoke. It's a celebration."

"If I may say so sir, I'm happy for you," Paul said.

"Thank you Paul. You had a big hand in it," Gregory said. "It's 5 o'clock now. We are heading over to Samantha's Aunt so I can meet her." Paul started chuckling at Gregory's announcement of meeting Aunt Elaine. "What's so funny?"

"Aunt Elaine can be a tough one Mr. Steele. She raised Samantha and loves her like her own daughter. She owned an advertising firm in her younger years and was tough as nails. I was employed by her for several years before coming here."

"Samantha told her the truth about our arrangement so she wanted to see us before our wedding," Gregory said.

"Just be straightforward with her and it will all be fine Mr. Steele," advised Paul.

"Am I interrupting?" Samantha stuck her head in the door.

"No we are just finished with the guest list for the party and I told

Paul I was meeting your Aunt tonight," Gregory said.

"I'll leave you both for tonight," Paul said. "Tell Aunt Elaine I send my best."

"I will Paul, thank you," Samantha said as Paul closed the door.

Gregory took off his jacket and poured himself a drink. Samantha watched as his muscles stretched across his back and shoulders. She also took off her jacket and sat on the couch rubbing the back of her neck.

"Do you want a drink?"

"No thanks," Samantha said. "Aunt Elaine said anytime after 6:30 was fine. She will have dinner ready for us at 7 o'clock."

Leaning down to kiss her hello, Gregory asked how the day was. After going thru the business part of her day as he would want to get an update on how things were in the PR part of the business, she told him about the party in the morning.

"The surprise shower was so much fun. Most of the gifts were lingerie," Samantha said.

"I seem to remember that you don't spend much time in lingerie or panties when you are with me or shall I remind you?"

"I am aware of that but maybe I should dress in flannels to protect myself from your amorous ways," said Samantha coyly.

"Trust me my love, you could wear a sack and I will still want you like I do now," Gregory said.

He got up to lock the door and turned down the lights. Turning on the stereo that was on the shelf, he tuned into an Easy Listening station.

"Come dance with me," coaxed Gregory. Extending his hand to her, Samantha went willingly into his arms. Laying her head on his shoulder, she caught his scent of cologne. It made her dizzy with wanting him. Swaying to the music together, he tipped her face to his.

"I want to make love to you Sam. Right here, right now." Samantha, with eyes glistening, started to take off his tie and opened his shirt one button at a time. She placed kisses on each section of skin that she exposed. Taking a deep breath by the hair on his chest, she lightly touched his nipples and then continued unbuttoning his shirt and placing more kisses right down to his belt buckle. Peeling his shirt off of him, she gently pushed him down on the couch.

Turning her back to him, she looked over her shoulder with a sultry look and started to unzip her dress for him. She pulled the dress slowly down her body, moving her hips in seductive movements. Gregory couldn't believe this was his VP of Public Relations and soon to be his wife. Turning to him, she moved her hands from her neck and played with her breasts thru her bra, making her way down her belly and putting her fingers into her panties. Samantha couldn't believe she was doing this either but something about Gregory made her feel so feminine that she wanted to share her soul with him. After touching herself and knowing she was ready for whatever he was going to do to her, she watched him intently as she reached back to unclasp her bra and let it drop to the floor. Kneeling down between his legs, she started to unbuckle his belt, unzip his pants and slowly pull them off of him. Running her nails up and down his erection that was still encased in his briefs, she started kissing and licking his stomach, going lower and lower, nipping at him thru his briefs. "You are mine," said Samantha as she freed his erection and took control over it. Moving her mouth on him, she was driving him insane. Not wanting to climax like this as he wanted to be deep within her, Gregory pulled Samantha onto the couch and started attacking her with his mouth and hands. Pulling the thong off of her, he buried his face between her legs, making her cry out in pleasure at what his tongue and fingers were doing to her. His tongue was driving her wild with a need to feel him inside her. That would be the only way to quench the fire they both started. Rising up over her, Gregory impaled her in one movement. Waiting for a quick second for her to adjust to him, he started to make love to her. Holding her face between his hands, he kissed her as she tasted herself on his lips. He wanted her to know how good she tasted, how he craved her. Wrapping her legs around his waist, he was able to go deeper into Samantha, giving her what she needed from him. Hearing her moan out loud was the sexiest sound to his ears.

"Tell me what you need Sam."

"You Gregory, I need you." Samantha grabbed his hair and pulled his face to hers for a searing kiss. Raising them both to greater heights with each thrust, Gregory felt Samantha go over the edge first and went faster to join her a few seconds later. Laying his weight on her, Gregory took a moment to catch his breath and emotions. He knew he was very attracted to her, couldn't get enough of her and maybe he was falling in love with her. Samantha was having similar feelings but she knew she was in love with him. Opening her eyes, she needed to look at him.

"You are something else Sam," smiled Gregory. "Have I hurt you?"

"No, it was perfect," she sighed. She was just about to tell him that she was falling in love with him but decided not to, yet anyway.

"I will never look at this couch the same way again," laughed Gregory. Samantha giggled with him and looked at the time.

"We have 45 minutes to get to my aunt's house and God forbid if we are late."

Chapter 13 Aunt Elaine

Pulling up in front of Aunt Elaine's house in the Maserati, Samantha's Aunt was sitting in a rocking chair on the front porch. She took note of Gregory getting out and walking around to help Samantha out of the car. In the back seat of the car, he reached in for a beautiful bouquet of flowers. Aunt Elaine witnessed a comfortable exchange between them and when her niece smiled up at Gregory, she just glowed. She knew then that they already slept together, probably several times. So much for the agreement her Aunt thought.

Samantha laughed out loud to something Gregory said. He laughed too and had the look of a man in love. Hand in hand, they came up the steps to see Samantha's Aunt.

"Hello Gregory, I'm Samantha's Aunt, Elaine Hartley."

Gregory extended his hand to her.

"I'm Gregory Steele Ms. Hartley; it's a pleasure to meet you. Samantha has told me so much about you. And Paul sends his very best."

"Ah Paul, I love that man. He's such a dear. He worked for me when I had my own business. Shame we haven't crossed paths before Gregory, you in publishing, me in advertising, but that was a decade ago. Hello my dear, you are looking beautiful. Come on in and make yourselves at home. My housekeeper made us a wonderful dinner so we can get to know each other and have a pleasant evening."

Handing her the flowers, Aunt Elaine thanked Gregory and asked Samantha to put them in a vase so she and Gregory could get to know each other.

Gregory looked around her quaint Colonial American house and saw some of the photos from different stages of Sam's life.

"You have a warm house Ms. Hartley. The antiques are beautiful and I especially love these photos of Sam growing up. "

"Thank you Gregory. I pride myself on antique buying, especially early American. The quality is so well made and it's our history, especially from this part of the U.S. Those photos of Sam are very precious to me. They are the only photos we found at her parent's home when they died."

Aunt Elaine paused for a quick second, thinking of her brother. Shaking herself out of her memories, she smiled at Gregory. "And please call me Aunt Elaine. You will be my nephew on Thursday. I'm planning on attending the wedding if I may."

"Of course," smiled Gregory. "We wouldn't have it any other way."

"So tell me, why the contract when it's obvious the both of you are attracted to each other? Why not let nature take its course?"

"In the beginning, it was purely a business deal. I didn't want an attachment of any kind until I started to get to know Sam. She is a very special woman and a very good employee for my company. This marriage was strictly for my business dealings," Gregory explained.

"That is until you started falling in love with her and her with you. I made be older but I'm not blind. I see very clearly this entire situation," said Aunt Elaine. "Listen; before Samantha comes back in here, I want you to know she means everything to me. I raised her to be a respectful, loving, kind, hard working young lady. She has done very well in your employ. I'm worried about the content of the agreement and worried about her feelings in all of this. I trust you will take every precaution to see that she doesn't get hurt if you can. She is not the type to be used and thrown away," warned Aunt Elaine.

"It was never my intention from the beginning and certainly not now after getting to know her. She is incredibly special and I will protect and care for her," Gregory said.

"And is there anyone else in your life that could affect these plans you have in place?"

"No, everyone else is ancient history. There is no one else but Sam."
Searching his face to find fault, she could find none. Nodding her head, Samantha chose that moment to come back in with the flowers.

"Gregory, these are beautiful flowers you picked out!" exclaimed Samantha. Looking at the both of them, Samantha put the vase on the table. "Is everything ok here?"

"Of course my dear, your young Gregory is quite a catch. You both make a beautiful couple. Now let's enjoy our dinner and celebrate your upcoming wedding," Aunt Elaine said.

The rest of the evening went very well, sharing childhood stories, questions answered about Gregory's family and his business. Aunt Elaine found him to be genuine with a good sense of humor and a brilliant businessman. He admitted that he was a little apprehensive in meeting her. Aunt Elaine enjoyed hearing that. Good to keep young men on their toes she said.

It was getting late and they had to get going. Kissing her Aunt goodbye with the promise to see her on Thursday, Gregory drove Samantha back to her apartment.

"My Aunt liked you," Samantha said.

"I really liked her too," said Gregory. "I love that she took care of you. That must have been a very difficult time for both of you." Too choked up to speak, Samantha just nodded her head in agreement.

"I have some business to do for the Italian merger tonight so I'll just head on home. That way you can get a good night's sleep," smiled Gregory.

Samantha knew what he was referring too and felt her face turning a nice shade of pink.

"I love that I can embarrass you a little Sam." Gregory raised her hand to his lips and kissed her palm. His touch sent shivers down her spine. Just that simple gesture made her want to explore him further but now was not the time.

"I'll be in early tomorrow to finish things up for Carlotta's tour and some other things. I took off Wednesday to move into your apartment and get settled in."

"That sounds good Sam. I figured we could go up to my estate on Friday and spend a long weekend there. My parents want to meet you too. We can relax up there and get to know each other better. At the end of the month is the party. We have a big few weeks coming up."

He pulled his car in front of her apartment and put it in park.

"You know, I plan on taking good care of you Sam. Never doubt that." Gregory lightly touched her cheek and moved his fingers across her bottom lip. Hearing her little gasp, he gave her a knowing smile and pulled her over to him. The minute her lips touched his, Samantha felt the familiar longing for more from him. Raising her hands into his hair, she pulled him closer to her so she could feel as much of his body that she could while in the front seat of the Maserati. As Gregory claimed her mouth, he felt the rush of desire surge thru his body. Licking her bottom lip, he felt her mouth open. He kissed her with such hunger that made Samantha breathless and whimper in her throat. Knowing that now wasn't the place to satisfy their needs, Gregory placed sweet kisses along her jaw bone and cheek.

"I'll see you in the morning. We have plenty of time to finish what we started," said Gregory. "Sweet dreams my Sam."

He waited until she got into her apartment.

While driving home, all he thought about was Samantha.

Chapter 14 Samantha

Early the next morning, Samantha labeled a few more boxes, packed additional clothes she wanted with her and tagged which furniture pieces she wanted the movers to take. Samantha knew she could come back and forth to pick up anything else she might need but this was good for now. Satisfied that this task was done, she got ready for work and got to the office by 8 o'clock. With her hair piled high on her head and held by a pencil, Samantha was so absorbed in her work that she had no idea that Gregory was standing by the door watching her.

"Well good morning Sam. Green tea I presume?" Walking over to her desk, he handed her the tea and leaned over for a good morning kiss.

"Why thank you Mr. Steele. You take such great care of your employees," flirted Samantha. "Especially when they are becoming my wife in two days," he said with a wink.

"I got up early and tagged furniture and boxes. I would love to bring my desk if I can fit it somewhere. I do work after hours too and would need someplace I could spread things out," Samantha explained.

"That's totally fine Sam. I want you to feel comfortable as this is your home too. How are you with all of this?"

"To be honest, I'm excited and scared at the same time," Samantha answered.

She leaned back in her chair. "I just want to help you to succeed with your business ventures and be a good partner for you this year."

Coming around to side of the desk, he knelt down so she could look at him.

"You have already surpassed all expectations of us being a success together. Let's just see where all this takes us," Gregory said. Unable to help but tease her, he added, "You know, not only are we great in the boardroom, we are fantastic in the bedroom." Feeling a blush in her cheeks, she knew this was a good time to ask him.

"I have been meaning to ask you why we haven't used any protection. Are we asking for trouble?"

"Always," said Gregory. Giving her that boyish grin, he gave her a quick kiss. "Have a good day and I'll see you later."

Samantha was frowning as he left with that statement. Did he want a longer commitment from her? Was he feeling like she was feeling? A baby! She was a businesswoman. She never thought about having a baby. Taking a sip of tea, she let her mind wander. It would be wonderful to have a little boy that looked like him or a little girl that looked like her. Her heart was doing little flip flops as she could be pregnant and not know it yet. What would she do after the year is up and she had a baby? Or did he want her as a partner for life? All of these questions were spinning in her head as Ronni bounced in her office. Flopping on the couch facing her, she noticed Samantha deep in thought.

"A penny for them?" Samantha looked at a Ronni and just told her what was bothering her. "We have been having unprotected sex."

"Really? I guess he wants to insure that when the year is up, you will still be with him. A baby will tie you both together. It wouldn't be so bad Sam. It's obvious you both care about each other, maybe even love each other. You just haven't admitted it to each other yet. That man doesn't take his eyes off of you for an instant."

"I did ask him if we were looking for trouble by not using protection." Samantha said.

"What was his answer?"

"Always was what he said," answered Samantha.

"There is your answer Sam. He wants a baby with you so are tied to him. Why don't you just relax and enjoy getting to know him," Ronni said. "Now, on your wedding day morning, there is a sunrise yoga class with that French instructor that we all drool over. We can welcome the day on a relaxing note and then I figured I would go back to yours and Gregory's place to help you get ready. I'll get ready there too. What do you think?"

"I say that is just perfect," answered Samantha.

"Ok, I'm off. I have a sales meeting in a few minutes. See you later." Ronni went over to give Samantha a hug.

"Don't worry about this. It will all work out," Ronni said.

What would I do without Ronni thought Samantha? Wondering if she were right about a baby, Samantha put her hand on her stomach. Would it be so bad to have his baby? Shaking that thought out of her head, Samantha tackled the work at hand.

The day sailed by. Not even thinking to stop to eat lunch, it was almost time to leave for the day. Seeing that it was one o'clock on the west coast, she wanted to check in with Carlotta and let her know she wouldn't be available for the next several days.

"It's going brilliantly Sam! I couldn't be happier. I will let Gregory know how wonderful you are for an added bonus in your Christmas stocking." Carlotta was a burst of energy the minute she saw that Samantha was calling her.

"I think I already have the bonus Carlotta. I move into his place tomorrow and Thursday is the wedding. We'll be heading up to Maine so I can meet his parents this weekend," Samantha said.

"How are you doing with all of this?"

"I'm excited and scared at the same time," explained Samantha.

"That's to be expected my dear. In the romance world we say live and let live. This marriage is starting off with an agreement but mark my words that man will be ripping up that contract in record time," Carlotta said.

Samantha hoped that Carlotta was right as she didn't think she could leave him after the year was completed. After she gave Carlotta the emergency contact numbers just in case she needed anything, Carlotta wished her a beautiful wedding.

"I wish you and Gregory all the happiness the world can give you Samantha. Trust in yourself and in Gregory. He will do the right thing. Enjoy and be the gorgeous Bride I know you will be," Carlotta said. "I'll see you both when I return."

Finishing up her call, Samantha gathered her things and said goodnight to Cindy who wished her congratulations again for her wedding on Thursday. She hugged her goodbye and started down to Gregory's office.

"He had an errand to make Ms. Hartley and said he would contact you later," said Paul when she approached his desk.

"Ok thank you Paul," Samantha said. "See you next week."

"Congratulations again and be happy," Paul said.

Samantha thought that was a little odd that Gregory didn't tell her that he was leaving early but then again, this was a business arrangement that has some exciting fringe benefits. Pushing any doubts aside, Samantha decided to do some shopping and see about buying Gregory a wedding gift. Even though this was a contract wedding, he has been doing a lot for her that she wanted to get him something really nice as a thank you. Going into a furniture store, she purchased a leather massage and heat recliner that he would love to replace the one that he had. With the stress he will be under with the expansion of his business, this would be a perfect gift for him. Setting up the delivery to also be on her moving day tomorrow, she was excited to have it there for him. She told them she wanted a big red bow on it too. Checking that off her list, Samantha went back to her apartment to relax. Deciding on a luxurious bubble bath to wipe the tension away, Samantha lit candles all over the bathroom, closed her eyes and started to relax. Her cell ringing brought her out of deep thought.

"Hmm hello," Samantha said.

"Hmm hello yourself," Gregory said. "You sound like you could be one of those sex phone 800 numbers. What are you doing?"

"I'm in the bathtub with candles and incense burning. I'm just relaxing in this nice wet water and I'm very wet all over, everywhere," said Samantha in her sexiest voice.

Hearing a groan from the other end of the phone, Samantha smiled.

"I wish I was there Sam, getting all wet with you," suggested Gregory.

"You could always get in your car and come on over here; I will make it so worth it for you," whispered Samantha.

"Oh my God," said Gregory under his breath. "You are killing me with this. You know I can't come over with all the work I have to do for the merger. Just for this, you owe me one and I intend to collect in full."

"You have a big tub at your apartment my love that we can share for many nights ahead," purred Samantha as she kept in character. "Would that be good for you?"

"You know you are good for me and to answer your question yes of course," Gregory said. "I'm looking forward to doing a lot with you Sam, more than you can ever imagine."

Chapter 15 The Big Move

Early in the morning, the movers arrived to take what Samantha tagged the day before. She loaded her own personal items which included her clothes, shoes, handbags and breakables including her favorite photos of her parents, Aunt Elaine and some fun vacation shots with Ronni. Samantha wondered if she would ever have photos of Gregory and her together. She would just have to make sure to take some so she would have them when the year was over. Pushing any melancholy thoughts aside, this was a new beginning for her, for now anyway. After everything was stored in her Lexus, she closed up the trunk just in time to see the Maserati pull in next to her.

"I thought you would love this!" Gregory said. He handed her a steaming cup of green tea.

"Bless you," said Samantha as she took a sip. "The movers are just about done so I just have to lock it up. Cindy already changed my mail for me so everything is taken of."

"Not everything," Gregory said. "Here are the keys to our apartment; here is your parking space number which is right next to mine on the right side. And this is for good luck." Gregory leaned down and kissed her. "I'm looking forward to having you as a roommate." He gave her that boyish smile that she already adored.

"I'm looking forward to it too," whispered Samantha.

"Ms. Hartley, we are ready to go," said the mover in charge.

"I'm Mr. Steele, if you follow me, we'll get you guys to the apartment. Sam, go ahead and lock up, we'll wait for you here,"

Gregory said. He was all business in getting everything settled from here on out and Samantha was grateful for his help.

Locking up her apartment, she met everyone by her car. Following Gregory, she was driving towards a new chapter of her life. She never thought that their relationship would escalate as quickly as it has but it just seemed so right and perfect. As they pulled up to the apartment, Samantha was brought out of her thoughts. She noticed the furniture delivery truck waiting out front too. Perfect timing smiled Samantha.

"Ms. Hartley?" The delivery man was standing there with his order form and clip board.

"Yes, that's me. Do you have what I wanted on it too?" Samantha asked.

"Yes Ma'am," as the delivery man opened the truck.

Gregory came over next to her.

"What's going on Sam?"

"It's your wedding gift from me," smiled Sam. Off the truck came a beautiful cocoa leather heated massage recliner with a big red bow on it.

"I can't believe this! I love it!" exclaimed Gregory. "I've always wanted something like this but never got around to buying one. I just have that old one." Hugging her close to him, he captured her mouth with his, showing promises of loving to come. He lifted his head to the applause of the movers and delivery men. Giving them a bow, he told them to get back to work and brought Samantha upstairs to the apartment.

"I figured you would want to tell them where to put everything," Gregory said.

"I have things in my car too for them to bring up."

"Give me your keys and I'll bring them, be right back," Gregory said.

Three hours later, everything was in place, her bed made, photos out on display. Samantha was putting the finishing touches away in her large walk in closet with a built in shoe rack. Coming up behind her, Gregory put his arms around her and rested his head on top of hers.

"That's a lot of shoes," he commented.

"Not really, considering I need pumps for work and shoes for evening wear and casual shoes. I picked up a pair of hiking boots for Maine too and sneakers for working out and slippers for yoga," Sam explained. As she folded her arms on top of his, Samantha was very satisfied with the organization of it all. She was also happy her wedding dress was all zipped in a garment bag so he wouldn't see it.

"Well Ms. Hartley, I made us some chicken salad on whole wheat bread for lunch. Care to join me?"

"I can't believe I'm marrying a man that is so very handy in the kitchen," Samantha said.

"And in the bedroom," said Gregory as he started kissing her neck. Doing her best to resist him, she was failing fast. Slowly turning in his arms, all thoughts of chicken salad went out the window. She wrapped her arms around his neck and hopped up to wrap her legs around his waist. He cupped her sexy ass in his hands and walked towards his bedroom. Banging into a few walls along the way made her giggle as he was kissing her. He also smiled behind his kiss, thinking how much he enjoyed making love to her. Finally finding his bed, he fell backwards which had her sitting on top of him. Unclipping her hair from the move, the chestnut waves flowed down past her shoulders. She slowly took off her tee-shirt, while slowly moving her hips on top of him. God she is hot thought Gregory. She started to unbutton his shirt and pulled it from his pants. Laying her hands on his chest, she lovingly touched his shoulders and biceps, down his forearms to his hands. Reaching up behind her, she unclasped her bra and touched each of her breasts to tease him. Gregory reached for the waistband of her jeans and unzipped them. Putting his fingers inside her panties, he knew she was ready for him. Moving her off of him, he removed the rest of her jeans and laid her on his bed. She looked a wanton Goddess lying there, anxiously awaiting her lover. He unzipped his pants, never taking his eyes off of hers.

Releasing himself from his briefs, his erection had a life of its own and it needed only Samantha. That thought startled him as he realized that he loved her. This brief time together, she worked her way into his heart and soul.

Today he would show her his love. Lying next to her, he lovingly kissed her while his hands explored all of her. He wanted to know every part of Sam. Moving his hand lightly across her stomach, she jumped at his touch at sensitive spots. Reaching her bikini line, she was wild with needing him. Running his fingers thru her curls, he teased the outer flesh before working his way in and out, going faster and faster until she moaned in pleasure when she found her release. Kissing her deeply, she had tears in her eyes from the sheer beauty of his giving to her.

"Don't cry Sam." Cupping his face in her hands, it was her turn to love him and love him she did. Laying him back, she kissed his neck and worked her way down with her hands, finding his sensitive spots. Watching his face to make sure he loved what she was doing to him, her hands kept going lower until it covered his erection. Smiling over at him, she kissed the entire length of him. Circling the tip with her tongue, she slowly put him in her mouth as she moved up and down him. He never took his eyes off of her as watching her love him was totally hot. As she started sucking on him harder, he moved himself carefully in and out of her mouth. Before things got too far, Gregory needed to feel himself deep within her so he pulled her up on top of him. She took him into her body while looking deep into his eyes. The feelings that were building between them were out of control. Faster and faster she moved until they both couldn't take it any longer. Sensing that he was near, she let herself go and he followed her, both enjoying each other at the pinnacle of their climax. Lying on top of him, she rested her head on his chest to enjoy this closeness.

No words were needed as they both shuttered from their release. Reaching for Samantha's hand, he linked her fingers with his. They had shared more in these moments than in days past. With tears in her eyes, several ran down her cheeks. Gregory gently wiped them away and kissed each cheek. This woman was so much a part of him now. Samantha sensed a change in Gregory, one of extreme caring bordering on love. His tenderness filled her heart with love for him. Smiling at him thru her tears, she gently touched his face, hopefully conveying to him how she loved him but was so afraid to say those words just in case he didn't feel the same towards her.

"I have an idea," Gregory said. "How about we just order a pizza and a movie for tonight? We have a big day tomorrow and we can get an early night."

"That sounds wonderful," said Samantha. "Ronni and I have sunrise yoga at 5:30 tomorrow and then she will be here to help me get ready and she'll get ready here too."

"5:30 yoga? I'll be rolling over and still be sleeping at that time. Just don't wake me up," Gregory said.

"I won't wake you up as I won't be sleeping in your bed tonight," announced Samantha.

"What? Can I ask why?"

"It's the night before our wedding and even though it's a contracted one, I don't want bad luck before our wedding," explained Samantha.

"I think I can hold out for one night and happy that you will be with me all other nights," said Gregory.

Kissing him with promises of magical nights ahead, Samantha was ready for dinner. So the night before their wedding, they shared a pizza while watching "Runaway Bride" with Samantha promising that she would not be like the Julia Roberts character and run away from the courthouse. As the movie was ending, Samantha kissed Gregory goodnight.

"I'll see you in the morning when we get back from yoga."

"Sweet dreams Sam. I can't wait until you are by wife."

True to her word, she slept in her room and Gregory in his with both of them longing to be in each other's arms instead of a wall away.

Chapter 16 Wedding Day

Samantha awoke fresh and ready for her sunrise yoga. Tip toeing out of the apartment with her mat, she was careful not to wake up Gregory. Ronni was parked out front and ready to go.

"Hey Mrs. Steele! Let's go greet the sun and the day!"

Feeling her heart do a little jump when Ronni called her that, Samantha was really looking forward to marrying Gregory. Smiling over at Ronni, she grabbed her hand and gave it a squeeze.

"Are you ok?" Ronni was searching Samantha's face for any hesitation in marrying Gregory.

"No, I'm just fine," answered Samantha. "This is really happening today and well, I'm fine with it."

"Good," said Ronni. "I have a feeling that everything will be just as it should be. Now let's get going before we miss seeing that gorgeous hunk of man teaching the yoga class." Samantha just started laughing at Ronni's carefree way. Driving down to the park, they saw that there was quite a large crowd gathered to start Sunrise Yoga.

"Guess other woman and some men like this French guy too!" bemused Ronni. "That chest and ass are worth battling these crowds, let's go."

"Oh Ronni, you are too much," Samantha said.

Laying their mats out, they went thru their moves in welcoming the day. This was a great way to start the morning for being grateful and thankful for a new beginning for everything and everyone in their lives.

"Geez Sam, look at his ass and abs. The positions he puts himself in: I didn't think that was humanly possible. What a badass with all those tattoos on his body too!"

"I agree," said the woman next to Ronni. "That's why I come here, more for the viewing than the workout. He could bend me in whatever position he wanted."

Ronni and Samantha both laughed out loud at the woman's comments.

The hour went by very quickly. As they were getting ready to leave, Sam saw a photographer taking their photo.

"Hey Ronni, someone just took our photo," Samantha said.

"Really, where is he?" Ronni and Samantha looked around the crowds but lost the photographer.

"Well, whoever they were, they are gone now. That seems strange and we should tell Gregory about it," Samantha said.

Getting into Ronni's car, Samantha wanted to make a quick stop.

"Let's stop at the market on our way to the apartment. I would love to pick up muffins and things to drink for all of us. I want to have things in the apartment as I don't know what Gregory already has there."

"Great idea, I could use a smoothie after yoga."

Back at the apartment, Gregory looked at his watch and thought that Sunrise Yoga should be over by now. Just as he was going to text her, a text came in from Sam that they stopped at the market to pick up muffins and things. He was anxious to see Samantha as he missed her in his bed last night. What was wrong with him? He was never like this with another woman. Hearing the buzzer ringing at his apartment, Gregory put down his cup of coffee he just poured and answered it.

"Who is it?"

"It's Mike," answered his brother.

"Come on up."

Gregory cracked the door open and went into the kitchen to pour another cup of coffee for his brother.

"Hey Greg! Where are you?"

"I'm in the kitchen. Come on in."

Both brothers hugged themselves and joked about Gregory getting married.

"So where is my lovely sister-in-law?"

"Sam and her best friend Ronni had Sunrise Yoga at 5:30 this morning. They are at the market picking up muffins and things and are on the way back."

"How are things between the both of you?" Mike already knew the answer but he wanted to hear it from Gregory. Gregory gave him the biggest smile.

"You are too much Greg. Just take things slow and get to know each other."

Gregory just smiled again.

"You are unbelievable Greg!"

At that moment, the door opened up to two laughing ladies. Samantha was carrying two bags of groceries, and Ronni carried her garment and overnight bag. They looked so adorable wearing their yoga wear with tight tank tops that left nothing to the imagination. Gregory got up to kiss Ronni on her cheek hello and then kissed

Samantha full on the mouth. "Hello my Bride," he whispered.

"Hello my Groom," whispered Samantha. Mike couldn't say anything as he just stared at Ronni.

Gregory noticed his brother's reaction to her.

"Um Ronni, this is my brother Mike, who is an attorney and therefore is never without words, until now," Gregory said.

"Mike, nice to meet you, I'm Veronica Tate, or Ronni like Gregory said. I work at the firm and am Sam's best friend." Frowning at Mike, Ronni looked directly at him. "Do you know you look like a young Robert Redford?"

That seemed to shake Mike out of his trance from just staring at her.

"I didn't know that Sam had such a beautiful friend," Mike said.

"You are just as charming as your brother," Ronni said. "Come on Sam, let's start to get ready. See you guys later."

The girls walked away with excitement about the upcoming day while Mike just stared.

Gregory slapped him on the back.

"That's what you come up with to say to Ronni? Where's my debonair brother?" laughed Gregory.

"I just wasn't expecting someone like her Greg."

"You better step it up if you want her to pay attention to you. She's one strong willed lady, says what she thinks and pretty outrageous at times," remarked Gregory.

"Noted, thanks for the heads up," said Mike smiling. Gregory hadn't seen his brother look this alive since the split before Mike's wedding. Maybe there was hope for him yet.

"Come on, let's get ready. We have two hours before our appointment with the judge," Gregory said.

So with the guys getting ready in Gregory's room, and the girls in Samantha's room, Gregory smiled at the laughter coming from their room. Not able to catch what was being said, he knew it had to do with Ronni being her crazy self while helping Samantha to relax.

Mike finished dressing before him and made his way into the kitchen for a bottle of water. He saw the refrigerator door open with two gorgeous legs and bare feet showing below the opened door.

Closing the door, Ronni jumped.

"Do you make it a habit of sneaking up on people unannounced?"

"No that wasn't my attention Ronni; I wasn't expecting you to be here. Can I get you anything else?" He watched her as he placed his jacket over the chair. Looking him up and down, she started walking past him and then stopped next to him.

"No, not yet," smiled Ronni. Then she started her way back to Sam's room.

She was going to have fun teasing him. This is going to be a great day.

Mike was speechless at her statement and with a slight smile, just stared at the sway of her hips as she walked away from him.

Ronni went back into Samantha's room, hopped on her bed and asked her about Mike.

"What's his story? Mike scared the Hell out of me as I closed the fridge door. He was just standing there looking at me," Ronni said.

"He's Gregory's older brother by two years, is a very successful attorney with his own firm downtown. He was engaged but split with her two months before the wedding. He is quite funny though I think he is attracted to you. Please be kind to him Ronni," laughed Samantha.

"I'll be kind. He asked me if I needed anything else and I told him, not yet," laughed Ronni. "I can tease him, can't I? That should be fun!"

One day thought Samantha, Ronni will meet her match. Now she was going to focus on getting that beautiful dress on and marrying Gregory.

"Please help zip me up," Samantha said.

When she all set, Samantha turned around so Ronni could see her. Hair upswept with a few curls trailing down her back, little rhinestone pins in her hair that caught the light when she moved, she looked like a princess. The dress was simple and elegant, with sleeves a little off the shoulders. She was a vision.

"Oh my God Sam! You are gorgeous."

Samantha grabbed Ronni's hands and couldn't thank her enough for everything that she had done for her. Ronni looked pretty amazing herself in a lavender silk dress that clung to her sexy curves and brought out the green in her eyes. Coming out of the room first, Ronni saw both men waiting for them. Both incredibly handsome, Ronni was quite taken aback when she looked at Mike. Something about him reached out to her. Shaking him from her mind, she concentrated on her friend and her wedding day.

"May I present the future Mrs. Gregory Steele." Gregory looked up to see Samantha as she exited out of her room and was just spellbound looking at her. He met Samantha half way as she walked into the living room.

"You are so beautiful Sam," Gregory said. Taking her hand, he placed a kiss there.

"I have something for you." Gregory gestured to Mike to give him the boxes. One contained the diamond heart pendant that they picked up at David and Mary's jewelry store. Gregory gently placed this on her neck while Ronni made sure to capture the moment on her cell phone. The next gift he let Samantha open. Inside it was the diamond beautiful tennis bracelet resting on black velvet that he bought for her.

"This is so beautiful Gregory, thank you so much." Tears glistened in her eyes as she looked up at him. He placed a sweet kiss on her lips before he helped her with the bracelet. Mike and Ronni looked at each other and smiled at the couple in front of them. Mike noticed tears in Ronni's eyes before she looked away.

"Shall we go?" Mike looked down at Ronni while extending his arm to her. Taking his arm, Ronni flashed him a beautiful smile that wasn't lost on Samantha.

"Yes and don't be startled if there are photographers downstairs. Word got out about our marriage so Paul took care of who was allowed to be on the scene for photos," informed Gregory.

"So that's who that was at yoga," Samantha said. "I saw someone taking Ronni's and my photo this morning."

"Hope he got my good side," Ronni said.

Mike leaned forward so only she could hear.

"I don't think you have a bad side," whispered Mike. Gaining a point in his favor, Mike loved that he made Ronni speechless. She definitely didn't have a comeback for that statement.

Ronni started thinking that he might be worth checking out and filed that thought away. Today was her friend's special day and she wanted to experience it with Sam. Sure enough, as the doorman opened the door, several photographers were there from the various media and publishing magazines.

Words of congratulations and give us a kiss where heard from the photographers. Gregory obliged them with a willing Samantha. Ronni and Mike stood to the side and watched the reporters snap their photos.

"Time to get going guys," Gregory said. He thanked the

photographers and turned to help Samantha into the waiting limo. Climbing in next to Samantha, he held her hand in his. Mike helped Ronni get in on the other side and seemed to sit closer to her than was necessary. Ronni didn't move away from him. She liked the feeling of being next to him. Michael put his arm across the back of her seat with Gregory and Samantha smiling at him. Michael winked back at the two of them, with Ronni oblivious of what was silently being said between the three of them. They headed downtown where they had a special appointment with the judge in his chambers for the exchange of vows instead of in a courtroom. Thanks to Mike, he pulled some strings to make that happen for his brother.

Arriving at their destination, another group of photographers were waiting for them. They walked up the stairs to find Aunt Elaine wearing a beautiful corsage on her lapel.

She kissed Samantha and had tears in her eyes.

"Gregory had this delivered to me this morning, my favorite orchid," Aunt Elaine told her.

Samantha looked at Gregory.

"So that's where you went the other day, you ordered my Aunt this corsage. Thank you Gregory."

"I have another surprise that I took care of that day too. You'll have to wait until later to find out," Gregory said.

Inside the courthouse, Mary and David were also waiting for them.

Hugging them both, Samantha was grateful for having the people they both cared about with them, if even they were getting married in the Judge's chamber and with a signed contract.

Chapter 17 Celebration

"I now pronounce you man and wife. You may now kiss your bride," said the Judge.

Gregory looked deep into Sam's eyes. He lowered his face to hers and gave her a tender kiss. Samantha wrapped her arms around his neck to deepen their kiss.

With applause in the room, they looked at everyone and just smiled. Samantha was glowing in love. Hugging her Aunt, they both cried happy tears. As Ronni hugged her friend next, she wished her all the luck and whispered to her that all will be great for them. Mike had his brother in a hug and then the photos between all of them started. Capturing everyone in a jovial mood, Samantha couldn't wait to get photos from everyone to put together memories to last her a lifetime. After signing the necessary paperwork, everyone exited the Judge's chambers.

"Ok, I have an announcement to make," Gregory said. Holding Samantha close to him, he let them all know his surprise.

"I'm inviting everyone to a special lunch at Mays Landing. They are waiting for us now for our reception," Gregory said. Everyone started clapping. It was a very exclusive restaurant right on the water.

"You planned this that day too. And Paul made it sound like it was an emergency," laughed Samantha. "It was an emergency. I wanted this to be a special day for you, for us. Let's go and celebrate our marriage," Gregory said. With the jovial group walking behind them, Gregory and Samantha celebrated their marriage with their families and friends.

As soon as they walked into the restaurant, Paul and his partner Charlie were there as well as Cindy and her husband Peter. Samantha was totally surprised as was the rest of the group. Gregory planned this in a few days and she loved him more for it. It was a beautiful lunch. Plate after plate of food arrived. Champagne and a special chocolate wedding cake finished off the reception. Standing next to Samantha, Gregory fed her a piece of the cake. It was pure chocolate Heaven! Taking a piece for Gregory, Samantha fed him a piece too. Reaching over to kiss her, they both tasted the chocolate icing that lingered on their lips.

"I could get ideas with chocolate, it tastes so good on you," whispered Gregory. Making sure that she was taking photos for them, Ronni was capturing all the candid moments. As she moved next to Michael, he smiled down at her and casually put his arm around her shoulders. Glasses started chiming as the crowd of well wishers wanted a kiss from the happy couple. As Gregory kissed

Samantha, he dipped her down over his arm, not taking his mouth from hers.

"Hey cut it out over there you two," shouted Mike. Actually, he loved seeing his brother so happy. He knew the minute he met Samantha that she was perfect for Gregory. Overall, it couldn't have been more of a perfect day to start their marriage. Saying goodbye to their guests, Samantha found her way by her Aunt's side.

"Samantha, you and Gregory make a beautiful couple. I wish you all the happiness that the world offers you. I love you my dear. Your parents are smiling down at you today and I know my brother would be happy." Aunt Elaine and Samantha just stood there hugging each other with tears of happiness on their cheeks. Taking her leave, Aunt Elaine said she would see them when they got back from their trip to Maine.

Ronni and Mike were waiting to go back to Gregory and Samantha's apartment to get their things and then they would leave the happy couple alone to start their lives together.

Chapter 18 A New Life

Once at the apartment, Samantha watched Ronni gather her things.

"What a day Sam! And I have a date."

"With Mike?"

"Yep," answered Ronni. "Do you believe this? He says things to me that throw me off guard. I like that. Let you know how things go."

Giving Samantha a hug, Ronni wished her a safe and fun trip. "See you when you get back."

"Thank you Ronni, for everything."

In Gregory's bedroom, a similar situation was taking place.

"So I have a date," Mike said nonchalantly to Gregory.

"You're kidding, with Ronni?"

"Yep. She's a sassy little thing but a softie. Saw tears in her eyes today and she got embarrassed when I saw her. There's a lot there that I'm going to find out about. Let you know how it all goes. Give Mom and Dad my best, safe trip," Mike said.

It was quiet and peaceful when they left. Samantha stood at the window looking out at the sunset, reliving the whole day when she felt Gregory come up behind and put his arms around her.

"A penny for your thoughts Mrs. Steele."

"I'm just watching the sunset and reliving our whole day in my mind. Thank you so much for the lunch with my Aunt and our friends. I'm sorry your parents weren't here," Samantha said.

"They are excited to see us tomorrow and have planned a party on Saturday for the family and their friends, just a big ole BBQ. Dad thinks he's an ace in the grilling department. I usually have to take over when he starts burning things."

"Sam and Mike have a date together too. I thought this might be a good match. They couldn't get out of this apartment fast enough," giggled Samantha.

"I guess they wanted to vacate the premises so we could continue our wedding celebration."

Turning around in his arms, Samantha brought Gregory's face to hers for a kiss of sweetness and love. She thought if this agreement is for a year, she would make it so maybe he wouldn't let her go. She didn't know how she would be ever able to leave him, never thinking that these feelings would run so deep.

Picking her up, Gregory carried her into his bedroom and gently lowered her to the floor without breaking their kiss.

Lifting his face from hers, Gregory turned her around so he could unzip her wedding dress. Kissing the side of her neck and every inch down her back as the zipper came down, Samantha closed her eyes and enjoyed the sensations he was giving her. Pulling the dress off of her, Gregory turned her back to face him.

"You are so beautiful my wife." Reaching up to undo his tie, Samantha slowly pulled it thru his collar while keeping her eyes connected with his. She then carefully took his jacket off and put that on the chair. Slowly unbuttoning his shirt, Gregory took it off and put that with the jacket. Bringing her close to him, he unclasped her bra and let her breasts touch his chest. Slipping her panties down off of her, his hands cupped her bottom as he lifted her up the ground. Samantha wrapped her legs around his waist as he carried her to their bed. Laying her down, he looked at all of her beauty, nothing went unnoticed by him. Taking off his pants,

Samantha sat up, holding her hand out to him. Clasping it, Gregory knew that his life had changed forever, that he would never let her go after a year. He only hoped she felt the same way. He had a year to show her his love so she would never want to leave him.

Moving her under him, Gregory entered her with one thrust. Samantha had her head back in pleasure. Kissing her exposed neck, his hand found her breast as he starting moving inside her. Samantha wrapped her legs around his waist so he could reach her deeper and deeper. Kissing each other, hungry for each other, his movements went faster and faster until they were both shuttering from the sheer pleasure of sharing each other. Gregory dropped little kisses on her face as she opened up her eyes to look at him. Touching his face and lips, he lightly nipped at her fingers. She loved these moments of pillow talk with him.

"Mrs. Steele, I have to say, you really know how to please your man."

"You are not so bad yourself Mr. Steele."

Feeling her eyes start to close, Samantha murmured to him. "Thank you for a beautiful day Gregory. I will never forget it."

"I won't forget it either." Pulling the comforters up over them, Gregory hugged Samantha to him and they both fell fast asleep. Early the next morning, Gregory got up before Samantha. He enjoyed looking at her while she was sleeping. He was a lucky man. This could have been a business match with someone he wasn't interested in and a boring year ahead. Samantha was an added bonus that changed everything for the best. Moving into the bathroom, he got in the shower to wake up for the 4 hour ride to Maine. Deep in thought and not hearing the glass door opening, Samantha stuck her head in. "Care for some company?" Gregory extended his hand out to Samantha. "

Chapter 19 On the Road

Turning onto Highway 95, Gregory set the cruise control to 75 and enjoyed the ride. Taking the drive up to Maine was a relaxing one for him as he had made this trip quite often and never got tired of the beauty surrounding him. He had spent hours thinking and planning his next business moves on these drives or made conference calls on the speaker phone. This time he could enjoy the time with Samantha.

"So tell me about your home in Portland," Samantha said.

"It's a peaceful place by the water. The house has five bedrooms, three bathrooms, 15 acres of land. There's a couple that live at the cottage about an acre off the main house. Antonio or Tony as he likes to be called and his wife Angelina have been with me since I purchased the house 2 years ago. They take great care of the house and the grounds. I love knowing that there are people watching it when I'm not there. I've notified them of our arrival so everything will be ready when we arrive."

"How far away do your parents live from you?"

"My parents are about 10 minutes from me, also on the coast but in a much smaller home. They thought I was crazy to buy it as it's quite large for one person. But now I have you," said Gregory as he smiled back over at her.

"I'm looking forward to meeting everyone, especially your parents." They both settled into a comfortable silence, listening to the 80's channel on satellite radio. Samantha couldn't keep her eyes open so thinking she would just relax for a few minutes, she actually dozed off for the next two hours. It's probably all the past excitement from the last two weeks. Her whole life has been turned upside down with everything moving so quickly. Gregory acknowledged to himself how good they are together and how he just wants to protect and take care of her. When did he fall in love with her and when do I tell her was the last thought on his mind when Samantha started to wake up.

"How long was I sleeping?" Samantha asked.

"About two hours."

"Really, I must have needed the rest. Sorry I haven't been much of a co-pilot here but I'm on duty now sir," Samantha said. Reaching for her hand, he brought it to his lips and held onto it.

"You are a very romantic man Gregory."

"I am but only with you Sam." Sensing he was going to say something else to her, the Bluetooth went off in the car.

"Hello Paul, everything ok?"

"Yes Mr. Steele. Hello Mrs. Steele. I trust you are enjoying your drive to Maine?"

"Yes but it's even more beautiful this time around," said Gregory. He smiled over at Samantha.

"I understand," said Paul. "I just wanted to inform you that congratulations are pouring in from colleagues in the business as well as the foreign companies emailing you. We have all yes confirmations for the party next Friday. They are all excited to meet Mrs. Steele and congratulate the both of you."

"That's great news Paul," Gregory said.

"I'm not finished yet. There are photos and write ups of the both of you in the various papers."

Upon hearing this, Samantha was all business. Reaching into the back seat of the Maserati, she pulled out her laptop, got a connection and started looking things up.

"Yes, I'm seeing them Paul. They even did some research on me and my background," Samantha said. "Look at this! They even brought up Aunt Elaine and her company."

"Your Aunt was pretty major in the advertising world, a force to be reckoned with. They look at you as someone that could walk in her shoes," Paul said.

"Thank you Paul," said Samantha.

"Have a great time with the family Mr. Steele. And Mrs. Steele,

Ronni told me to tell you that we have lift off, whatever that means," Paul said.

Clapping her hands, Samantha started laughing.

"Thanks Paul. I got it. Ronni is just too much."

"Ok Paul, I'll find out from Samantha what's going on. Thank you and enjoy your weekend." Pressing the off button, Gregory asked, "Care to fill me in?"

"It seems as though your brother and my friend are hitting it off just fine. Mike will never be the same again," Samantha said.

"Mike could use some shaking up and she would be the one to do it. His fiancé did a number on him. She didn't tell him she wasn't totally divorced yet and this was two months before their wedding. Mike hasn't let a woman in until Ronni. He told me he had a date with her coming up but I didn't think it would happen so fast. That's going to be another story. We are still writing ours," said Gregory.

"I seem to know another Steele brother that moved very fast."

"When you know it's a good thing, you don't wait. Sam, you are the best thing that has happened to me, contract or no contract. I just want you to know that," Gregory said.

"The same for me too Gregory," Samantha said. Not quite an "I love you" but Samantha would take it. Coming around the corner, Gregory started slowing down.

"We're here!" announced Gregory. Samantha looked up from her paperwork and closed it all up. Now was time to enjoy the long weekend with her husband and get to know him more.

Driving down the long driveway with tall pine trees on either side, they came to a clearing. Right in the middle of the clearing was a beautiful colonial mansion with a huge porch across the front and big columns.

"This is gorgeous Gregory," said Samantha in awe. "This place must be magnificent in the winter."

"There are three working fireplaces in the house, one of them is in the master bedroom," said Gregory. "I think you will love the back of the house. It has a deck with a built in fire pit, in the ground pool and a Jacuzzi, all overlooking the water. I think this will be a nice mini honeymoon for us," said Gregory. Parking the car in front of the house, Gregory grabbed their two leather weekend bags and Samantha grabbed Gregory's leather briefcase and her laptop carry bag.

"Hello Mr. Gregory!" shouted Tony. "Hello Mrs. Gregory, Welcome to Whispering Pines!"

"Thank you Tony. How have you been? And Angelina?"

"Oh we have been fine. We are so happy that you found this beautiful lady. Mr. James already called me to see if we heard from you," Tony said.

"Ok, thanks Tony. I'll give him a call. Sam, want the twenty-five cent tour?"

"I can't wait. Please lead the way," said Samantha. "It was nice to meet you Tony!"

Walking into the house took Samantha's breath away. The foyer had vaulted ceilings and skylights. The open floor plan showed windows across the back of the house that overlooked the deck and the bay. The living room has plush cream couches with colorful pillows adorning them. French doors opened onto the deck. Walking into the kitchen was a culinary dream. Granite countertops in shades of brown, cranberry and cream coupled with cherry wood cabinets was so elegant. The center island was fully functional with a sink too. Steel appliances finished off the look of the kitchen.

To the side was a formal dining room with the same rich cherry wood furniture and taupe colored walls with crown molding. On the other side of the living room was a den that had a full home movie theater and big leather recliners. It also had a powder room near the front entrance.

At the top of the winding staircase were all of the guest bedrooms and another bathroom. The last bedroom at the end of the hallway was magical. Facing the entire back of the house, it had its own balcony with two beautiful chairs and a table on it. The four poster king size bed was the focal point of the room. The working fireplace was across from the bed with a flat screen TV above the fireplace. The adjourning master bathroom had his and her sinks, sunken Jacuzzi bathtub, all in mauves and cream colors.

"Gregory, the whole house is so beautiful, I understand why you would buy it, just look at the view. I'm sure every season is a painting from here," Samantha said.

"Now I get to share it with you," said Gregory. "Why don't you go and unpack us while I call the folks? Mom is probably out of her mind to meet you and to finally have a woman in the family to combat all the testosterone," Gregory said.

"Sure thing, I will get to it," said Samantha.

As Gregory disappeared downstairs, Samantha heard him talk to his Dad.

"Hey Pop, we're here." Turning to their overnight bags, she got everything unpacked in record time. Sitting down for a moment to gather her thoughts, it was going to be a test ahead meeting his parents. No matter what happens, she will treasure these moments with Gregory. Live and let live was what Carlotta told her and she was doing just that.

Gregory calling up to her broke her out of her thoughts.

"Hey Sam, my parents are coming over with dinner. Mom thought you might be tired and would want to just relax in your new home. They should be here in 20 minutes."

"Ok, that's great. I'm done up here so I'll be right down."

Going into the bathroom to freshen up, she changed into a light blue cashmere sweater. Even though it was June, it gets a little chilly up in Maine at night. She was grateful for the fireplace in the bedroom to take the chill out of the room. What romantic nights they could have there too thought Samantha.

Heading back downstairs and into the kitchen, she found Gregory opening a few bottles of wine.

"What can I do to help?"

"Well, for starters, I want you to come here so I can properly give you a welcome to Maine is for lover's kiss," said Gregory with that boyish grin of his.

"I didn't know that Maine had a Maine is for Lover's slogan. Thought that was only for Virginia?" Gregory circled his arms around her.

"Maine, Virginia, how about wherever you and I are, we create our own love slogan?"

"I think that sounds like a brilliant idea," said Samantha as she raised her face for his kiss. Before he claimed her lips, he smiled down at her. All was lost in the moment when his lips touched hers. Teasing and demanding, Gregory already knew what she loved and how she responded to him.

"Um excuse me son. Let the poor girl breathe," said James Steele as he carried in three bags of food. "Your mother has made enough food to feed an army as she wanted to make sure the fridge was stocked the whole time you are here."

As much as his Dad complained, he absolutely adored Gregory's Mom. He just needed to complain about something in his retirement years.

Coming over to the both of them, he hugged his son and then looked at his new Daughter-in-Law. James saw the elegance and sweetness in Samantha. He did some research on her background and also her life. He knew about her family and knew of her Aunt too in the business world. For such tragedies she had growing up, Samantha paved her way in his son's company and was a good partner for him. Strange that Gregory never spoke about her until two weeks ago. Letting it drop from his mind, he wanted to meet her too.

"Welcome to the family Samantha," said James. He gave her a big hug and a kiss on the cheek. "Thank you very much Mr. Steele."

"Stop right there young lady, you better call me James or Dad but none of this Mr. Steele stuff. Ok?" James gave her a wink.

"Ok," said Samantha.

"Where is she?" Gregory's mom couldn't contain herself as she entered the kitchen. She was so excited to meet her new daughter in law.

"How are you Mom?" Holding his arms out to his Mom, she breezed right by Gregory.

"I can hug you in a second; I want to meet my new daughter-in-law Samantha." Looking playfully rejected and seeing his Dad laughing to himself, Diana went to embrace Samantha.

"The daughter I've always wanted, welcome to the family."

Samantha and Diana both had tears in their eyes during this emotional meeting.

Gregory and his Dad opened two beers and were just watching the exchange.

"Son, I think we are both in trouble here. Women are starting to take over in numbers."

"Oh hush James. You know I've always wanted a daughter. Come here my son and let me give you a hug too. You have made a beautiful choice."

Samantha watched this exchange and saw where both Gregory and Michael got their looks from. Gregory was the exact image of his Dad, and Michael was fair like his Mom. They were so lucky to have each other. Samantha was going to enjoy this weekend.

"Ok men, out of the kitchen. Samantha and I are going to put dinner together for all of us so I can get to know her. You go talk somewhere else."

"Sure Di," laughed James. "We know when we aren't needed; try not to grill her too much, ok?" Giving her a kiss on the cheek, Samantha saw that he gave her a little pat on her backside and thought how very sweet. Now she knew where Gregory gets his romantic gestures from.

"Come on Pop, let's head out on the deck and let the ladies get dinner all set," said Gregory.

"More like let's get out of here before they put us to work," laughed

James.

"Oh ignore them Samantha. I have quite a few different things here as I didn't know what you liked," explained Diana. She brought out a tub of pulled pork, her own mom's recipe, and lobster salad made from this morning's catch, homemade clam chowder and blueberry muffins too. Samantha was ravenous just smelling everything.

"This is amazing Diana," Samantha said. "I would love to know how you make the lobster salad; it's one of my favorites."

"Here, taste this." Diana gave Samantha a spoonful of the lobster salad.

"This is Heaven," sighed Samantha.

"It's Gregory's favorite too," Diana said. "So did you and Gregory meet at the office?"

"Yes, he came down to meet the Senior Staff and as his Vice-President of Public Relations, I was one of the staff he had a meeting with and the rest is history."

"I'm so happy that he met you. Gregory needed someone that could be his partner in life and add to it, not ruin him," explained Diana.

"If you are trying to find out if I know about if his previous engagement, the answer is yes," Samantha said. "My Aunt was the one who actually told me, Gregory hadn't said a word about her."

"Your Aunt was the one who raised you, right?"

Samantha was helping put the plates on table and smiled at Diana. "Yes, she is my Father's sister. She took me in and raised me as her daughter. She never married, she was married to her business," explained Samantha.

"Well I can see how our Gregory is in love with you and I'm so happy that you are now a part of our family," said Diana. Giving Samantha a quick hug, she motioned to her husband and son to come in to eat.

"Let's go call in the men. James will complain less on a full stomach." Outside a different type of question and answer session was happening.

"So why is it you never spoke about Samantha son?"

Here comes the grilling I wanted to avoid thought Gregory. He took a big gulp of beer before answering.

"Well Pop, thinking of how the first engagement didn't go as planned, I kind of kept things to myself." James looked at his son like a prosecutor would. He sensed that something wasn't right here.

"This all happened very suddenly, oh I know your mother is thrilled with this marriage, I think there is something else here. Is she pregnant?"

"Not that I know of," Gregory answered.

"Do you love her son because this is the type of girl that deserves that from you, not that other one, whatever her name was."

"Alex," supplied Gregory.

"Yes Alex, she wasn't worthy of you."

"Yes Pop, I love Sam," answered Gregory. Feeling good to finally say it out loud to someone was a relief. Now he had to figure out when to let Samantha know.

"Ok son, looks like our women are coming out to get us. Hope you're hungry. Your Mom brought a lot of your favorite things." Throwing his arm around Gregory's shoulders, they met the ladies at the door and went in for a delicious meal.

Enjoying dinner together, Samantha was comfortable meeting her in-laws and loved hearing stories about Gregory and Michael growing up. Since James knew some things about Samantha already, he didn't grill her like Gregory thought he would. Helping himself to another scoop of lobster salad, Gregory loved seeing Samantha getting along beautifully with his parents. The food of course was the best as always too.

"That was amazing Mom," exclaimed Gregory.

"Really Diana, everything is delicious," added Samantha. "I also want to thank you for teaching Gregory how to cook. I really enjoy him cooking for me on some nights." Gregory leaned over to Samantha and gave her a kiss on the cheek for saying that.

"I made sure both the boys know how to cook and do their laundry, especially to be there to help their wives when they start having babies," Diana said.

Samantha got a little pink in the cheeks and Gregory just smiled at his Mom. She was not subtle at all in her wish to become a

Grandma.

"Ok my dear," James said. "It's time to leave the love birds alone now. We have plenty of time to visit tomorrow."

"Mom, we'll clean up. Everything was wonderful and we are so happy to be here this weekend," Gregory said. "We'll be over in the morning as I want to take Samantha around the area."

James came over to hug his son and then hugged his new daughter-in-law.

"Welcome to the family again Sam," said James.

"Thanks Dad," Samantha said. That was the first time she used that word since she was a little girl and James knew that. Noticing the tears in her eyes, he squeezed her hand and waited on the porch for his wife.

"Bye my dear," Diana said. "We are going to have such wonderful times together."

"Thank you Mom," said an emotional Samantha. Gregory put his arm around Samantha as they followed his Mom out on the porch.

"The BBQ starts at 2 o'clock," James said. "I have a few new recipes to try out on everyone."

"I'll be ready to take over Pop," laughed Gregory.

"Good to see you happy Gregory. Good night Son."

They watched his parents get into their car and drive off.

"Your parents are so wonderful Gregory," Samantha said. "You get your business savvy and your romantic notions from him."

"I'm getting a few romantic notions that I would love to share with you right now,"

whispered Gregory. Reaching under her sweater, he caressed one of her breasts. "Do you know how crazy you have been making me all night?" Slowly moving his hand from under her sweater, Samantha ran into the kitchen. Gregory just laughed and locked up the front door. Then he stood in the kitchen doorway and watched her move around the kitchen like she has been there for years.

"I have a kitchen to clean up and want to put things away," Samantha said.

"Ok, I have a little work to do right now so I'll see you upstairs," Gregory said. Giving Samantha a kiss on her head, he went upstairs but not to work. He only used that as an excuse. He lit a fire in the fireplace and filled up the Jacuzzi tub. Putting on the R+B station, "Let's Get It On" came on the radio. A little Marvin would get anyone in the mood thought Gregory.

In the kitchen, Samantha heard the radio go on and the bathtub getting filled. He's not working at all but working on other plans. She smiled to herself as she could work on a few of her own plans. After she finished putting away the dishes, she grabbed two glasses and a bottle of wine. Two can play at this game. Shutting off the lights, she started up the stairs as Gregory was singing the words to Marvin Gaye's hit. Quickly taking off her sweater and jeans, Samantha shook her hair so that it was sexy and full. She stood in the doorway with her most seductive pose wearing just her bra and panties.

Gregory came out of the bathroom in black silk pajama bottoms and stopped short looking at her. She was a vision to him.

Samantha walked into the bedroom and placed the bottle and glasses on the side table. Walking up to him, she reached out her hands to his forearms and moved up them to his shoulders. Moving her hands over his chest and then down to the front of his pajamas, she felt his erection coming to life under her hands.

Gregory slowly turned Samantha around and started kissing her on her neck. His hand unclasped her bra and he let it fall to the ground. Holding her breasts in both hands, he thought they felt fuller than usual and loved feeling her reaction to his touch. Moving to her panties, he put his hand inside them, moving his fingers against her.

Feeling waves of passion building in her, she whispered "Please Gregory." Turning her to face him, he knelt down in front of her, slowly pulling her panties down and off of her. Placing kisses on her lower abdomen, he moved his lips lower, following where his fingers were going. When Gregory reached between her legs, Samantha had to lean on him as she didn't have the strength to stand any longer. Putting her one leg around his shoulder, she opened herself to Gregory's lips as he kissed her at her core. Gregory was using his tongue as he moved his fingers deep inside of her. Samantha grabbed onto his hair to pull him closer to her. She felt herself come apart at his touch while crying out his name in passion.

"Please Gregory," sobbed Samantha. Picking her up, he carried her to the Jacuzzi tub and placed her in the water. Quickly shedding his pajamas, he joined her in the tub and pulled her on top of him. Samantha lowered herself onto him. Just being one with him was overwhelming; the pleasure building was almost too much to bear. Throwing back her head, Gregory kissed and licked her nipples as he pushed harder into her. Shattering into a million pieces, Samantha found another release. Gregory held on as long as he could and joined her in their pleasure. Kissing her deeply, Gregory thought she was her most beautiful during their love making.

"Mrs. Steele, you are going to kill me if you keep riding me the way you do," laughed Gregory. Turning around and leaning back against his chest, Samantha sighed peacefully as she became totally relaxed. The jets of water lovingly touched both of their skin. Taking the sponge and some bath wash, Gregory started rubbing the sponge across Samantha's breasts, down her stomach between her legs. Moving the sponge up and down, Samantha couldn't believe that Gregory stirred such strong emotions in her that she wanted him again.

"What do you say we get out of here and sit by the fire with the wine you brought up?"

"Sounds wonderful," said Samantha.

Gregory got out of the tub first and wrapped a towel around him. Holding his hand out to Samantha, he helped her out of the tub and wrapped her in a big fluffy towel. Taking her hand, they went back to the bedroom, where Gregory grabbed the glasses and she grabbed the wine. Noticing that Gregory had a comforter on the floor by the fire, they sat side by side. Pouring two glasses of wine, Samantha laid against his chest with Gregory resting his head on top of hers. Each sipping the wine, the comfortable silence and the crackling logs made for a romantic evening.

"This is really beautiful Gregory, these last few weeks of being with you and everything. It's been really special. I'm looking forward to seeing the area and especially the lighthouse."

"We'll take a drive around so you can see everything," Gregory said. "But now, I want to make other beautiful memories with you."

Taking their glasses away, Gregory laid Samantha in his arms with the reflection of the warm glow of flames on her face. Looking down at her, he moved her curls away from her face as he caressed her baby soft cheek. Gregory knew this was the moment to let Samantha know what's in his heart.

"I love you Sam. I want to have a full life with you, no contract, no holds barred. Children everywhere, expanding business and you right by my side. You are my wife and I'm never letting you go."

Samantha felt the tears roll from the sides of her eyes as he professed his love to her.

"Gregory, I fell in love with you from the first night at my apartment. I was so afraid these last few weeks that after the year, you would let me go. I've wanted to tell you how much I love you but was so afraid," admitted Samantha.

Gregory lowered his mouth to hers and thoroughly explored it. Opening her towel, he brought his head to her breasts, kissing and licking them as her nipples rose to meet his mouth. He trailed his hand between her legs, moving his fingers inside of her, making her ready for him. Moving between her legs, he made her one with him. Moaning in pleasure, Gregory started moving inside of her.

He was making love to her, from the depths of his soul to her heart. As Samantha wrapped her legs around his back, Gregory was able to go deeper into her. She was in the throes of passion with each thrust he did to her. The feelings were crashing down around them as they moved towards the sweet release that only Gregory could give to her. Reaching the heights together, they slowly calmed down with their legs and arms wrapped around each other. Gregory rested his head on her forehead. Samantha wiped the sweat from his face and kissed him sweetly. "I love you Gregory. You are my life. I could never be without you," said Samantha.

Chapter 20 Exploring

Waking up alone in the bed, Samantha didn't know where Gregory went. Wrapping the sheet around her, she stood at the balcony door to take in how beautiful the bay was. The lighthouse could be seen all the way from the house. She was looking forward to explore the trails that she could see from the house that lead to the bay. Then she relived last night in her mind, the love they professed to each other and shared. This was a new day and beginning for the both of them.

Hearing footsteps coming down the hallway, Gregory walked into the bedroom carrying a breakfast tray of scrambled eggs, toast, two glasses of orange juice and some fruit. In the center of the tray, there was a bud vase with some wild flowers from the garden.

"Here you go my Bride, some breakfast as you must be hungry after last night's activities." Giving her a wink, Samantha just shook her head at how adorable he was.

Gregory looked so handsome to her with his bare chest and black silk pajama bottoms. She realized how very lucky she was to have a man like this to call her husband and how wonderful things were turning out.

"I'll join you on the balcony in a few minutes. I just want to freshen up a bit," Samantha said.

Gregory got everything set up outside on this gorgeous summer morning. Reaching for the paper on the tray, he opened it to the business section and just drank some orange juice while waiting for Samantha.

"Don't wait for me," Samantha yelled out.

"Its fine, I'm just reading the paper," answered Gregory.

Samantha came out of the bathroom wearing the white lace little shift nightgown which left absolutely nothing to the imagination. She made sure to show off her curves in front of him to her best advantage. Reaching in front of him for her orange juice, she made sure he got a clear view of her breasts before she sat across for him. Stretching like a cat, she sexily put her feet up on his chair near his lap. Putting the newspaper down, his eyes looked at his sexy wife.

"Are you trying to get pregnant my dear?" He started caressing her ankles and slim calves. Chills went right thru her body as he touched her. Deciding to get up and sit next to him, she took one of the strawberries and bit into it. The juices started running down her chin. Taking his finger, Gregory wiped the juice on it and put it by Samantha's mouth as she started to lick it. Then she took his whole finger in her mouth and started sucking on it. Narrowing his eyes at her, she took another strawberry, and standing up, she straddled him feeling the hardness already come to life. Placing the strawberry in her mouth, she leaned forward. Gregory closed his mouth on the other half of the berry, eating it until all that was left was Samantha's lips. Pushing past them, their tongues met, entwining together, teasing each other and making them want something more from each other.

Gregory fondled her between her legs as she whimpered against his lips. Knowing what she needed, he opened the front of his pajamas.

Samantha rose up a bit and then joined him as he thrust hard into her. He needed her, needed to mark her as his, this was pure sex. Samantha arched her back and opened herself wider to him as he pulled her shift away from her breasts and took one nipple into his mouth. Grazing it with his teeth, Samantha cried out with how good he was making her feel, so alive, every fiber of her being was alive. Moving her hips seductively on his lap, Gregory needed more of her. Faster and faster she moved until Samantha felt his fullness erupt inside of her that made her join him on their side of Heaven. Resting her head on his shoulder, he lifted her face for a gentle kiss on the lips. Threading her hands thru his hair, she brought his mouth to hers. Finishing their love making with sweet kisses, Gregory pulled up the lacey front of her shift but not before lightly caressing both of her nipples.

"You know Mrs. Steele, there is nothing more I would love to do but to stay in bed all day with you but we are requested to be at the BBQ this afternoon."

"And you made such a lovely breakfast too," said Samantha as she slowly moved off his lap. Pulling the chair closer, Samantha scooted next to him while eating a piece of toast. "Ok tour guide, what's the plan today?"

"I want to take you over by the lighthouse, there are good trails there, you brought your hiking boots, right? The trail leads to the beach area so that would be a great place to see everything. I'll think we'll have time to go into town so you can see the stores, and then we'll change and head over to the folks for Dad's famous BBQ. How does that sound?"

"Wonderful. I'll get moving now, I can be ready in 20 minutes," Samantha said. True to her word, she was downstairs, ready to go wearing a light pink tee-shirt, form fitting jeans that fit her curves beautifully and her hiking boots. Her hair up in a pony tail, she looked fresh and lovely from their morning love session. As she was finishing cleaning up the breakfast dishes, Gregory came in wearing tight jeans, black tee-shirt and hiking boots. Hair still damp from his shower and obvious he didn't shave this morning, Gregory couldn't have looked sexier to her. Smiling at him, she turned her attention back to the dishes but not before he saw those blue eyes of hers acknowledging her attraction to him. We are going to take this time to really get to know each other thought Gregory as there are no problems in the other part of our relationship. Smiling to himself, he looked at how her jeans clung to her, just everything about her suited him. Who would have thought this could happen just from an idea of a contracted marriage. Gregory made a mental note to call his brother about the contract and to destroy it.

"Are you ready to go Sam?"

"Yes, I just have to grab my bag and we can go."

"Oh and I called my parents telling them of our change of plans this morning that we wouldn't have time to come by this morning but would see them at 2 o'clock." Turning slightly pink as now his parents realized we were in bed this morning, Gregory started laughing.

"It's ok Sam, they know we are on our weekend honeymoon, it's to be expected," Gregory said.

Laughing with him, they headed out to the lighthouse and to enjoy the day.

Waving to Tony who was getting ready to mow the yard, they got into the Maserati and headed to the coast. Opening the sunroof, Samantha sat back in the seat and looked at all the landscaping around her. The rocky coastline with the sandy beach below held such beauty. About a ten minute ride to the lighthouse, Gregory pointed out little things to her about the history of the area. Samantha was really enjoying the stories as they arrived at the lighthouse. It had black and white stripes from the ground to the top so it could be visible for the sailors at sea. Pulling into the parking lot, Samantha and Gregory grabbed their sunglasses and 2 bottles of water that Samantha had safely tucked away in her bag. Holding her hand as they were walking to the lighthouse, Gregory started to tell her a story about this particular lighthouse.

"You know there is a folklore story about this area about two people madly in love that ended in tragedy."

"Really, how does the story go?"

"Well, there was a local fisherman who was so in love with this young girl. They were destined to be married but he wanted to take one more voyage out in the open waters to bring in a good catch. Seeing him off from those shores down there, a storm came in and destroyed most of the fishing boats and killed the crews that went out that day. This young lady waited all day and night, standing at the shores edge for her beloved to return. Seeing destroyed ship boards coming onto the shore, she thought her beau had died so not being able to live without him; she stepped out into the water and drowned. Finally her love was able to make it back to shore and upon finding out that she drowned herself thinking that he had died, he couldn't live without her and he drowned himself in the same waters. Meeting together in Heaven, they were never to be separated again." Gregory looked at Samantha as she looked at the sea.

"Come on, I know the store owner. I want to pick you up the full story and other folklore that you can read." Opening the door, the bells rang, alerting the store owner of another customer.

"Well look at this! Gregory Steele, your Dad said you were up this weekend with your Bride. This must be her!"

"Sam, this is Charlie Winters, store owner, local fable teller, lighthouse keeper and Santa Claus at the mall at Christmas".

"So nice to meet you Charlie," Samantha said. "That's quite a full resume you have there."

"It keeps me busy Sam, especially at Christmas, that's my favorite part. So, what can I get you folks?"

"I was telling Sam about the fable of the young lovers and the sea and wanted to buy her a book of that story as well as a few others."

"I have what you want right here Greg." Handing him a paperback of local Maine folklore, it contained that story and a few others that were popular in the area."

"Gregory told me the story Charlie, it's quite sad, don't you think?"

"Well I think it has another moral to it, that true love stands the test of time; that if there is true love, it will last forever." Nodding her agreement, Charlie reached on the shelf for a small book for her. "A wedding present from me to you," Charlie said.

Looking down at the small book, it contained just that story and love poems written by local authors in that area.

Gregory came over to see what they were talking about.

"Thank you Charlie," said Sam. She leaned over to kiss his cheek. "Congratulations to the both of you. Take your time shopping, there's a lot of fun stuff here. All proceeds go to the preservation of the lighthouse and to keep these stories alive in the years to come." Gregory put his arm around Sam and lifted the book from her hands. Seeing what it was, he looked down at her and kissed her forehead.

Smiling up at him, Sam announced that she wanted to look around the store. She wanted to shop for Aunt Elaine, Ronni and pick up something for Michael and their parents.

Charlie was right; there were good items in the store. She picked up a beautiful crochet table runner for her Aunt, made by Charlie's wife, two comfy hoodies with Maine's logo on it for Ronni and Mike and found a beautiful table cloth for her new Mom that she had to get for her. She found a beautiful photo essay book of their area of Maine, shots taken from animal life to the lighthouse to the ocean. It was beautifully done and thought that her new Dad would love that. Gregory agreed that his parents would love the gifts that she didn't have to buy for them but she wanted to. For Gregory, she found a warm hat and cashmere gloves in black of course that he could wear when the cold months came. She helped Charlie wrap all of the items and thanked him again for the book. He thanked them for helping support the lighthouse as they left the store for their next stop. Storing everything in the truck of the car, they started out on one trail that Gregory was familiar with. The views were amazing and knew that Sam would really love it. It was where he came to meditate and be one with the creator of all beauty. It never ceased to amaze Gregory the beauty of each season here and wanted to share all of that with Sam.

"There is a lookout spot up ahead that I think you will enjoy Sam. Let's stop there." Walking a few more feet, Samantha started hearing the ocean wave's crash on the shore.

"Ok, stop here and close your eyes," commanded Gregory. "Let me guide you to the spot and I'll tell you when to open your eyes."

Holding both of her hands, Gregory guided her to the rails.

"Open your eyes now."

Samantha's voice caught in her throat at the sheer beauty of it. On the steep cliffs to the left of her, waves were crashing onto the rocks, sending white foam in the air. A grassy field with wild flowers dotted the landscape in front of her. Sand dunes rose to the right before the ocean where the waves came in. She watched the sandpipers dodge the waves while trying to eat what they could.

"Thank you Gregory for sharing this special place with me."

Samantha made a mental note to definitely come back here when she could.

Realizing what time it was, they needed to get home to get ready for the BBQ. They didn't have time that day to go exploring in town. They would have to do it the next time they came up to Maine. On the drive home, Samantha started reading one of the folklore stories from the book that Charlie gave her. It was her second home now and she wanted to soak up the history that surrounded it.

Pulling into the driveway, Samantha grabbed the gifts while Gregory went to speak to Tony about some of the landscaping. Telling her that he would be right back, Samantha let herself into the house and went to get ready. Seeing they had about an hour before they had to go, Samantha jumped into the shower as she thought about the wonderful day she had with Gregory. She really loved the area and was looking forward to the picnic.

Getting out of the shower in record time, she put on mascara and lip gloss, dried her hair and deciding to keep it down, with the chestnut waves curling down her back.

Standing there in her bra and panties, Gregory came in to take his own shower.

"You look beautiful Mrs. Steele," as his eyes looked at her from top to bottom. Adding some more lip gloss, she licked her bottom lip while looking at him. He couldn't contain himself when she looked at him like this. "Sorry love, this is going to be a quickie."

Thoroughly letting her know how much she affected him, Samantha melted into his embrace as his lips crushed down on top of hers. Carrying her into their bedroom, he laid her on their bed and started to kiss her from her breasts, down her stomach until he got between his legs. Teasing her with his tongue, he brought Samantha to her ultimate pleasure. Calling out his name to please come to her, Gregory didn't hesitate. Pulling her to the edge of the bed, Gregory thrust himself into her. Moving in and out of her, Samantha couldn't believe the feelings that Gregory stirred within her. Gregory leaned over her, sucking on her bottom lip and moving down to breasts while Samantha cried out in pleasure. Unable to hold back any longer, Gregory brought them both to relief together, sharing their love once again like the young lovers that had died for each other.

Chapter 21 BBQ

Gregory and Samantha arrived at the BBQ a half hour late as his mom looked at them with a smile on her face. She relived the memories of when she first married James; he couldn't keep his hands off of her. She was pregnant with Michael before she knew it. Gregory was so much like his Father and with Samantha as beautiful as she is, Diana was sure she would be a Grandma sooner than later. James came over to his wife wearing a "Kiss the Cook" apron and holding a cooking fork in his hand.

"That son of ours is losing his head and all sense of time with his wife," James said.

"Oh hush James. Don't you remember that when we were first married, you practically chased me around the house for a solid year," said Diana laughing.

"And I would still chase you now but these knees aren't what they used to be," chuckled James. He was kissing his wife as Gregory and Samantha joined them.

"Hey Pop, let her up for air, ok?" laughed Gregory. He couldn't help but give some of the teasing back to his Dad.

"Don't you look beautiful Sam in that sun dress! You are glowing," Diana said.

"Thank you Mom," said Samantha. Kissing both of her in-laws, she told them that they bought them a few surprises.

"Why don't we go into the house and let Gregory and his Dad figure out the food cooking detail? The troops here are getting restless with hunger." Samantha and Diana left the men to the cooking. "Want a beer Pop?"

"Sure," said James. "Is there something on your mind son?" James had an uncanny way of knowing things before they happened. He called it the anticipation of being a Prosecutor his whole life, to always be one step ahead.

Gregory thought this was as good a time as any and told his Father about the contract he had with Samantha, right down to each detail, and that Mike had drawn up the agreement. His Father just stared at Gregory; truly not believing what both of his son's cooked up together in regards to Samantha.

"Now that is the most idiotic thing I have ever heard of and that your brother drafted the thing up, well that's not why he has a law degree and his business! What the Hell is the matter with both of you!" said an irate James. Flipping some burgers and chicken before his reputation as burning the food became a reality once again, he had some questions for his son.

"Ok, do you love her and does she love you? Does anyone else know about this so called agreement? If word gets out about it, I can't even begin to think about the consequences for your business." Gregory cut his Father off.

"Yes, we both love each other and no one else other than Paul, Samantha's Aunt Elaine and Samantha's friend Ronni knows about it. They are all trustworthy people."

"Michael needs to destroy it immediately and you need to speak to Samantha about that being done. Gregory, thank you for telling me. I knew something was not quite right from the beginning. For starters, you have never spoken about her and for someone getting married, one would think you would tell your parents," James said. "Not a word of this to your Mom. Please tell Samantha the same. Saying that I'm disappointed in the both of you is an understatement and I will definitely speak to Michael about his incredibly stupid part in all of this.

Now let's feed the hungry troops here and enjoy the afternoon."

Inside the house, Samantha helped Diana put her new tablecloth on their dining room table. "It's gorgeous Samantha! Thank you," said Diana. "James is going to love the coffee table book too. It was incredibly thoughtful of you to do this." Getting a little teary eyed, Diana held Samantha's hand. "I'm going to miss you when you leave tomorrow. Make a promise that you will come back up soon. Gregory gets so absorbed in his work that sometimes the visits aren't as frequent as we would love."

"I will Mom," Samantha said. "I have fallen in love with this place; I promise we'll be back soon."

Together they went back outside to enjoy the BBQ. Diana

introduced her to the family and friends that came to celebrate.
Gregory couldn't take his eyes off of his sexy, sweet wife. When she
held his cousin's baby, he felt a tightening in his chest on how
beautiful that image was. Someday, she will be holding our baby
thought Gregory.

"You're on your own for now Dad. I'm going to have lunch with my
wife," Gregory said.

Samantha saw Gregory coming towards her, as she handed the baby
back to Gregory's cousin.

"Everything ok?"

"Yes, I just want to steal you away from these ladies and show you
something."

"Now that sounds promising," whispered Samantha. Taking her
hand, they filled up their plates and Gregory guided her to the
gazebo that faced the woods. "Having a good time?"

"Yes of course. Everyone is so sweet and wonderful. You have a
good family Gregory," acknowledged Samantha.

"Thank you," said Gregory. "I told Dad about the contact."

"What? Did he get mad about it?"

"Well, he wasn't pleased. He advised us to rip it up and not to tell
my Mom."

"Of course, we don't need that anymore. Probably wouldn't have
needed it from the beginning either," Samantha admitted.

"Oh really?"

"Yes," Samantha said. "I started caring for you the minute I saw you, well that and literally falling at your feet. I'll make arrangements about getting rid of my apartment too." Reaching out to touch his face and bottom lip, Gregory held her hand by his mouth. As he looked deep into her eyes, he kissed the palm of her hand and each individual finger. Shivers ran down her spine at the feelings Gregory was creating. Leaning towards him, she craved his kisses, his touch. Tracing her lips with his finger, he covered her mouth with his own. Trying to keep his desire for her in check, he slowly moved away from her.

"Grab your plate before things get out of control," Gregory said. "Let's head back to the party."

The rest of the afternoon passed quickly by. From socializing, the family volleyball game, talking business and planning the next picnic, everyone had a great time and grateful that James didn't burn the food. As the last guests left, it was time for Gregory and Samantha to leave for home too.

"Well Mom, Pop, we are going to get going too. We are leaving early tomorrow back to Boston," said Gregory.

"I hate this when you leave," said Diana holding both of their hands.

"I promise. We'll be back up soon Mom. Thank you both for everything." After saying their goodbyes, they headed back to house to enjoy their last night in Maine.

Chapter 22 Samantha

Reaching the house, there was a beautiful full moon overhead, bathing the grounds in a silvery light. Samantha felt sad that they had to return to Boston tomorrow, back to the craziness of their jobs and life. She loved spending this time alone with Gregory but was excited to see Ronni and catch up with her. They hadn't spoken the whole time they were away and she wanted to know what was going on with Mike. She made a mental promise to get them both back up to Maine sooner than later, maybe with Ronni and Mike too.

"Would you mind if I get some work done Sam? There are a couple of things that I have to answer before we get on the road tomorrow," Gregory said.

"That's fine," Samantha said. "I'll clean things out of the fridge and pack what we don't need right now." Kissing her on top of her head, Gregory headed to his den and got involved with his work at hand. Finishing up with the kitchen, Samantha headed up to their bedroom. Changing into her white silk men's pajamas, she climbed into bed with the book that Charlie gave her. Not being able to keep her eyes open, Samantha fell into a deep sleep. She saw herself in a dream, waiting at the shore for Gregory to come to her. Calling out to him, her voice was lost on the crashing waves. Then she saw him in the distance, walking towards her. He was calling to her too and trying to get to her. Out of the shadows next to

Gregory, walked a woman, a tall, sexy brunette with her hand on his arm, coaxing him from Samantha. Not able to resist this woman, Gregory turned and walked away from Samantha. No she cried watching Gregory walk away from her. Not being able to live without him, Samantha walked into the waves. She was tossed around in the dark sea until she disappeared from sight.

Yelling out loud from upstairs, Gregory ran out of the office, taking the stairs two at a time to get to Samantha.

Running to her side of the bed, he pulled her to him she as lay sobbing against him.

"What's wrong baby," said Gregory. He wiped her hair from her face and the tears from her cheeks. "I'm here." Gregory just hugged Samantha in his strong arms against his chest, his heartbeat a soothing rhythm to calm her down.

"I had such a horrible dream. Before I went to sleep, I was reading the story about the young lovers. I was by the sea, calling for you. You were coming to me until a beautiful woman came and pulled you from me. It was your ex-fiancé and you went with her. I stepped into the sea to die as I couldn't live without you."

"Ok Sam, it was just a dream. There is nothing to remotely worry about with Alex. You are my life, my love. She is a calculating woman and my worst mistake. That's why I don't talk about her to anyone. I would rather forget she ever existed," said Gregory. He held Samantha's face in his hands. "Never doubt for one minute my

feelings for you which get stronger as each moment passes."
Samantha looked at him with tear spiked eyelashes. Biting her
bottom lip, she felt new tears well up in her eyes at Gregory's
profession of love for her.

"Now Sam, you can't look at me like that without me making love to
you. You drive me insane." Pulling Samantha to him, he crushed
her lips beneath his, his hunger growing by the minute. He needed
to possess her, heart, body and soul, to chase any doubts she might
have about the dream she had.

Samantha grabbed for Gregory's shirt, pulling it over his head, came
back to his mouth, entangling her tongue with his, teasing and
demanding at the same time. Laying her down on the bed, Gregory
ripped open her satin pajama top and with his mouth, pulled and
sucked on her nipples, driving her wild with the need to have him
inside her. Mumbling against her lips that he would buy her a new
pair of pajamas, he needed Sam. Reaching to her pajama bottoms,
he pulled them off and settled his mouth between her legs, as she
grabbed his head to pull him in closer. Higher and higher she rose
as Gregory's tongue tortured her, making her cry out with needing
him. He continued his assault on her until he felt her whole body
shutter with an earth crashing release. He wanted her to feel his
complete love of her, to share with her how wonderful it can be.
Looking up at him with love in her eyes, he slowly unbuckled his
belt. As he pulled his pants off, Samantha eased her hands down

the full length of him. Placing her mouth on him, Gregory held onto to the post on the bed. He didn't know how long he could hold on with what her mouth was doing to him. Licking and sucking him, Samantha moved her hand down the length of him as she kissed the top of him. Climbing onto the bed, he leaned back on his legs, pulled Samantha up to his waist and impaled her with one thrust. Opening her legs wider for him, Samantha gripped his shoulders, her nails digging into his skin. Moving on top of him, he wanted to him to feel her love, to give all that she is to him. With his mouth moving to her nipples, she arched her back into him as she felt her release coming soon. Feeling her getting tighter around him, he knew she was near and held out for as long as he could. "Come for me Sam, let yourself go," Gregory whispered against her ear. That was her undoing. Wrapping her arms tight around him, she cried out his name against his neck.

Faster and faster, they climbed together, reaching the pinnacle that lovers reach together, only to cascade down with sheer pleasure in each other. He held her face between his hands and kissed her long and hard. Laying her down next to him, he moved some of her hair from her face.

"You are not like anyone Samantha; we belong together," whispered Gregory as he held her in his arms.

Chapter 23 Road home

With the car all packed, Gregory locked up the house as they said goodbye to Tony. Last night was a turning point in their relationship. Reliving in her mind what Gregory did to her made her sigh in the front seat.

"Are you ok?"

"Yes fine," said Samantha. She smiled up over at Gregory as he got into the car.

Reaching for her laptop, Samantha logged into her work emails. Putting her hair up in a pony tail, she got down to the business at hand; helping her husband run his company.

"Carlotta emailed me about the successful tour she had. She sends us congratulations and wouldn't miss the party at the end of the month," Samantha said. "It's the event of the year! There's also an email from Ronni; sales from Carlotta books are up by 60 percent internationally. I think her next tour should be a few countries in Europe."

"Find out from Ronni her heaviest sale volume and some of the not so great markets too. Maybe we can come up with a strategy to build up her secondary markets. Is there anything else?"

"There's an email from Aunt Elaine. She's looking forward to seeing us at the party and hoped we had a great time in Maine. Here's another one from Ronni. She and Mike are having a good time and that he's a sweet guy," said Samantha.

"That sounds promising," agreed Gregory. "It will be good to get home."

Four hours later, Gregory parked the Maserati in his parking spot. Grabbing their bags, the doorman welcomed them back with congratulations and their mail. There were some gifts there too from some friends and business partners.

Gregory put their bags in the apartment while making her stop at the front door. Coming back to get Samantha, he picked her up and carried her over the threshold.

"Welcome home Mrs. Steele." Kicking the door closed with his foot, he slowly lowered her to her feet while kissing her. She started giggling behind her kiss.

"What's so funny?" He looked down at his adorable wife.

"That was very Clark Gable of you, forceful, sexy and romantic all at the same time."

"Well frankly my Dear, I would rather have you in my bed doing more than just kissing," admitted Gregory.

Samantha batted her eyelashes at him. "Well maybe Sir, I just may allow that, but right now, I have things to do."

Heading to the bedroom to unpack, she dialed Ronni's cell.

"Sam! How I've missed you! How's married life treating you?"

"It's wonderful, he's amazing," Samantha said. "I wanted to see how you are doing with Mike."

"Everything is wonderful. We've been having a great time. He's funny, smart, he gets me. Listen, he's coming by for dinner. Let's have lunch tomorrow to catch up."

"Ok, sounds like a plan. I can't wait to see you." Wishing her a good time with Michael, Samantha thought she would turn in early. After the long drive back and the full weekend they had, she was tired from the whirlwind last couple of days. Sticking her head out the door, she saw Gregory immersed in work. Not wanting to bother him, she took a quick shower, and crawled between the sheets. Within minutes, she was fast asleep. It was midnight when Gregory got caught up on all of his work. Realizing that Samantha was nowhere to be found, he peered into their bedroom and found her fast asleep. Taking a quick shower, he set the alarm for seven o'clock and slid into bed next to her. Pulling her next to him, thoughts of loving her in his life filled Gregory's heart.

Monday morning dawned on the muggy side. With it being summer in July, it was to be expected. Samantha noticed that the dress she put on was a little snug thru the bust area but didn't think anything about it other than she should cut back on some of the food she was eating and maybe having salads the next few days.

Grabbing green tea in the cabinet, she had a little but it seemed to make her a bit queasy. Finding a can of ginger ale, she felt better drinking that. Waking Gregory, she told him she was going in early and would see him later. She didn't want the staff to think she was given any special favors now that she was married to the CEO.

Samantha really loved her job and did it well. She wanted to keep the trust and respect of her co-workers.

Getting to the office at eight o'clock, Cindy was waiting for her with open arms.

"I'm so glad you are back. It was a beautiful wedding and reception. Mr. Steele really surprised all of us," Cindy said. "And you look beautiful Samantha. Marriage agrees with you."

"Thank you Cindy. He's pretty amazing."

Settling into her work schedule, Ronni decided to make her appearance known.

"Hello married lady!" Giving Samantha a big hug, she noticed a slight change in her.

"Have you put on weight, your boobs are huge," commented Ronni.

"I thought my dress was a little snug." Just then a wave of nausea came over Samantha. "I think I'm going to be sick." Ronni grabbed the garbage can and helped her friend. Samantha sat back in her chair as Ronni tied up the bag to get rid of it.

"Stay right here, I'll be right back."

"I'm not going anywhere," said Samantha.

Samantha started thinking about her cycle and when her period was due. That day had come and gone. It wouldn't surprise her that she was pregnant. They never took any precautions. It could have happened that first night of them being together. Samantha wouldn't doubt it and it seemed about right with the timing.

"Here, eat these crackers and drink this Coke. It will settle your stomach," Ronni said.

"Thank you Ronni," said Samantha.

"Don't thank me. It took every ounce of will power not to throw up next to you after witnessing that."

Samantha started laughing.

"Ronni, I know I'm pregnant. We haven't used any protection and Gregory, well, he's like you said, a demanding and giving lover, many times over," informed Samantha. "Ronni, are you blushing?"

"Well, that's a little more information than I need to know about," laughed Ronni. "Pick up a pregnancy test on the way home and schedule an appointment at the doctor this week. I have to go. Let me know how the test comes out." Giving her a hug goodbye, Samantha was left with her own thoughts of an impending pregnancy.

Chapter 24 Blue

Samantha picked up a few pregnancy kits just in case she messed up doing one of them. As she was waiting for the test results, she had mixed feelings. One was a natural anxiety over what a baby would do to the both of their lives. The other feeling was of extreme happiness knowing that they might have created a beautiful life together. It took her breath away just thinking of it. As the five minutes was up, she glanced over at the test. Not only was it blue, it was bright blue! A feeling of overwhelming joy and protectiveness came over her that Samantha just leaned against the sink as tears came flowing down her face. Putting the test back in the box, she thought that she would hide it in her dresser drawer until Gregory came home. She wanted to tell him when they were together and not when he was in the office. Then Samantha made an appointment with her doctor for Friday morning, the day of the party so that was set. She wanted to take all precautions that the baby was healthy and that how she was feeling right now was totally normal. Thinking about the party on Friday night, Samantha glanced over at her closet and started biting on her finger. The black dress! And was it going to fit her right now? Samantha quickly took off her jeans and her top. As she walked over to the closet, she stopped in front of her full length mirror to look at her body. Turning to the left and then to the right, she really didn't notice anything different in her stomach area but her breasts! They definitely look a size larger. Liking that new look and thinking that Gregory would too, Samantha smiled as she grabbed for the black dress. Slipping it on, Samantha was very happy with the overall look. The new weight gain in her breast area made the dress even more stunning on her. All she would have to worry about was not getting sick while wearing it. Placing her hand on her belly, Samantha was getting used to the idea that she was having Gregory's baby. Smiling at the thought of if she were having a girl or a boy, her cell phone started ringing. Seeing it was Gregory, she figured that he was going to be at the office late tonight with the merger in the final stages of completing.

"Hi Sam. I have a last minute dinner meeting tonight with the Italian company that we are merging with. I won't be late as their owner says he doesn't want to keep me from my lovely bride."

"I understand Gregory. Good luck and I'll see you later."

Samantha was looking forward to telling him about the baby but now it will have to wait. Making herself some soup, she did some research on being pregnant. Reading about the first trimester, everything was as it should be. She wished her mom were alive to share all of this with her and to answer all the questions that were swirling in her head. For now, the internet and her doctor would be there for her. Closing her laptop from sheer exhaustion, Samantha took a shower, put crackers in her night stand drawer with a can of Coke for the morning and fell into a deep sleep. She never heard Gregory come in at eleven o'clock. Getting undressed, he slipped into the bed and pulled her over to him.

"Gregory, I didn't hear you come in," whispered Sam. She was so exhausted, she couldn't even open her eyes.

"Goodnight my Sam."

Waking up feeling a little queasy, she did what Ronni told her to do. Eating some of the crackers and drinking some Coke, Samantha felt a little better so she got out of bed. Going into the kitchen, something caught her eye under the front door. Seeing it was the morning paper,   Samantha thought it was strange as they didn't receive the paper like this. She picked it up and saw the headline "Socialite and Millionaire Ex: a possibility again" with a small photo of Gregory and another woman. With trembling fingers, Samantha turned to the gossip pages and saw a photo of Gregory with Alexandra Whitley on his arm. As Samantha clutched the end of the counter, she looked at the photo of them walking side by side. Feeling the bile rise to her throat, she just stared at the image before her. How could this happen? Samantha felt her emotions get the better of her as she stifled a sob behind her hand. Hearing a text coming in on her phone, she saw it was from Ronni.

"WTF" was all that Ronni wrote and it was Samantha's sentiments exactly. What was going on here? She left the papers open to that page and went in to get dressed as she just wanted out of the apartment. Samantha didn't know where she was going to go; she just didn't want to see Gregory. She needed to get control over her emotions and to figure out what her next plan of action would be. Now she had a baby to add to this situation. What a complete mess if he was back with Alexandra! Right now, she needed to get away from Gregory and figure out what she should do.

Chapter 25 Samantha

First things first, Samantha thought that she would call Paul and let him know that she wouldn't be in the office today. There was no way she could face everyone that she worked with as the headline of the paper was emblazoned on her mind. Feeling a tear move down her face, she dialed Gregory's office number and Paul picked up immediately. It was though he was waiting for her call.

"Paul, its Sam. Please let Gregory know that I won't be in the office today. I really can't deal with the paper headline right now and if there is any truth to it."

"Now Mrs. Steele, you know that witch staged everything. There is no way Mr. Steele would have anything to do with that woman. And you have to know I would never put you in this position if another woman was still in the picture."

"I don't know Paul; they looked very cozy in that photo. What do you expect me to think when I see that? I'm sorry but I really don't want to talk about this right now. It's all a mess and I don't know what the Hell to do about it. How could he do this to me? The whole staff probably is wondering what is going on. Now I just want the day to think things through." Samantha was trying to be brave but was dying inside. Hearing Paul start to say something else, Samantha hung up on him. Driving downtown, Samantha heard her cell ring. Seeing it was Ronni calling, she picked up the phone.

"Sam, oh my God, are you ok?"

"As good as I can be. I'm headed over to my Aunt's house to spend the day there." Samantha just decided that as she was speaking to Ronni.

"Listen; give Gregory a chance to explain. I spoke to Michael when I saw the headline. He was looking at it too when I called him. I believe he called Alexandra a bitch and thought for sure this was all staged. Listen Sam, I know you are upset. From what I know of her she's a conniving, evil woman. She did the ultimate sin to Gregory, there is no way he would ever want to be with her, not when it's so obvious he loves you."

"Ronni, I don't know what I'm going to do. This is a huge mess and on top of it, I am pregnant. Please don't tell Michael. "

"Of course I won't tell him. This will all work out, I'm sure of it. There has got to be a simple explanation to all of this. Gregory loves you, anyone can see that."

"I need time Ronni. I just pulled up in front of my Aunt's. I'll call you later."

Getting out of her car, Samantha saw her Aunt standing on the front porch waiting for her. What Samantha didn't know was that Paul already called her as well as Gregory. Listening to the both of them, Aunt Elaine knew that what they told her was the truth about the photo and the article written about Gregory. She asked Gregory to calm down and to come by around lunch time. She would have things taken care of on her end with her niece to help get them back on track.

Running up the stairs, Aunt Elaine opened her arms to Samantha as reached the porch. Tears fell from Samantha's eyes as she felt comfort being in her Aunt's arms.

"Now Sam, this will all be ok. I'm here for you. Stop your tears and let's talk about everything but there is one thing I have to do. Not everything is as it seems."

Frowning at her Aunt, she saw her dialing the phone, hoping it wasn't Gregory she was calling. Feeling her emotions all over the place, she wasn't ready to speak to Gregory just yet.

"Peter Collins please." Not knowing what the response was to her Aunt's request, Samantha definitely knew who Peter Collins was. He was the Editor in Chief of the paper that ran the photo and article about Gregory. What the Hell was her Aunt up to?

"I don't care that Peter is in a meeting. Get him out of the meeting and tell him it's Elaine Hartley on the phone."

Looking at Samantha, she put the call on speaker phone so Sam would be able to hear the conversation she was looking forward to have with the editor.

Hearing Peter pick up the line, he sounded overly bright as he asked her, "Elaine, how are you?"

"You know damned well how I am Peter since you spoke to me yesterday. But what you don't know is that I'm pissed as Hell at the photo op and article written about Gregory Steele this morning."

"I don't understand Elaine, why you would be pissed as Hell over this."

"Don't patronize me Peter! That is my niece's husband you had your cheesy writer and photographer do an unfounded story on."

"Oh shit," said Peter quietly.

"I'm sorry, what was that?"

"I said shit Elaine."

"Precisely," said Aunt Elaine. "So this is my question to you. Did they even research the story before putting that crap on the front of my paper? Do you realize how totally incorrect this story is? I've received the inside scoop myself. Your photographer snapped the photo as Alexandra was being tossed out of the restaurant. She grabbed Gregory's arm as she was being escorted out of there and there are plenty of witnesses that will attest to that. Are you trying to bring a lawsuit down on me and the Board of Directors?"

"Oh my God," was all that Peter could say. So Aunt Elaine continued her lecture.

"This is what you are going to do. You are going to have that writer, Tom Williamson I believe, write an apology and a retraction as well as the rookie photographer write his apology and have it in tomorrow mornings paper. Please tell Tom I'm incredibly disappointed in him. I have been following his news reporting but this trash is so beneath this paper that if it happens again, he and his partner will find themselves without a job in this town, do I make myself clear? And that goes for you too Peter. It's your responsibility to make sure that the articles are checked out and to the truth as possible."

"I'll handle it Elaine."

"Have a good day," said her Aunt as she hung up the phone.

Facing her dumbstruck Aunt, Samantha finally found her voice.

"You own the paper?"

"Fifty-one percent of it and I can guarantee this is how the Board of Directors would want this all handled. Aren't you going to ask how I know about this?"

"That thought has crossed my mind too."

"I spoke to Paul and then your husband this morning before you arrived here. Paul has been a trusted employee and friend to me for the past twenty-five years. He knew what happened and coupled with hearing your distraught husband, I knew that this entire scenario was a set up. Taking care of the paper and getting a retraction was first and foremost to getting everything back on the right track. So, dry your eyes my dear and make yourself presentable. My lunch date will be arriving in five minutes and so will your Gregory. I don't think you want him to see you like this."

Giving Samantha a sly smile, she just shook her head at her Aunt.

"You are a badass Aunt Elaine, do you realize that?"

"I don't know about a badass but no one screws with my family. I like to keep my hands in the business so to speak." Hearing the doorbell ring, she pointed in the direction of the bathroom and went to answer the door.

Seeing her lunch date standing there as well as Gregory pacing on the porch, she invited the both of them in.

"Where's Sam?"

"She's the bathroom, freshening up. I think you will find that things are on the right path now Gregory. Just don't screw it up with Samantha. She is still a bit confused over everything. I did what I needed to do for the both of you."

When he was just going to ask what she meant by that statement, he saw Samantha walking back into the room, Gregory just wanted to hold her but knew that they needed to talk things through first. He was just so happy to see her.

"So Samantha, we are going to lunch. Do you have the spare key?"

Shaking her head yes, her Aunt told her to make sure she locked up when they left. Hugging Aunt Elaine and thanking her, Samantha closed the front door and faced Gregory. Walking over to her, Gregory held her hands in his.

"Sam, you know that this was all made up. You know damned well how I feel about that bitch and that she orchestrated this shot. They didn't write about what happened next. That shot was taken as I was escorting her out the front door. When the photographer snapped the photo, she happened to grab my arm to make it look like we were together. The owner threw her out of the restaurant.

You can ask the businessmen that were there with me last night. She was up to making trouble for us and I can see that she has. Please Sam, you have to believe me. You have to believe how much I love you." Seeing the hesitation in her eyes killed him.

"Please Gregory; I need time to get all of this in perspective." She tried to pull out of his arms.

"Fuck perspective! You can't honestly believe that I would even be with this woman after you have spoiled me for all women!" Taking hold of Samantha again, he forced her to look at him. Seeing the tears stream down her face, Gregory reached up to wipe them away. "You are my entire life, everything that I do, everything that I am; is all for you Sam. There is no way in Hell that I would ever give you up. I knew that from the first day I met you. To even think for a moment, after everything that we've shared, that I would be remotely interested in that bitch or any other woman, makes me insane. In case you haven't noticed Sam, I am deeply in love with you, only you. I don't know how else to tell you, but I can damn well show you."

Pulling her against him, Gregory possessed her mouth with a passion that surprised the both of them. Running his tongue across her bottom lip, she opened her lips to let him in. Hearing him groan deep in his throat, Samantha met his kiss with all barriers pushed aside. Feeling his tongue enter her mouth, Samantha met him with the same passion and love that it was starting to overwhelm her.

His hands moved down her back to pull her hips close to him so that she felt his erection thru her jeans. She knew that as their passions started to flare up, her Aunt's house was not the place to do anything about it. Feeling Gregory lips move down her throat, he hugged her tightly to him.

"We'll have to continue this at home later," whispered Gregory. Nodding her head in agreement, Samantha touched his cheek as her emotions got the better of her.

Turning his face into her palm, he kissed it sending shivers down her body. Picking her up, he placed her on his lap on the couch.

"Your Aunt said something about taking care of something for us. What did she do?"

"Well, unknown to me, she owns fifty-one percent of the paper that printed that photo and article and was the ultimate badass as she ripped that Editor in Chief to shreds on the phone. There will be a retraction and an apology printed in tomorrow mornings paper. "

"Remind me never to piss your Aunt off. Can we move forward from this Sam? You know I would never do anything to hurt you."

Putting her arms around Gregory, she just hugged him. She knew that she had to tell him about the baby.

"Gregory, I have something to tell you." Sitting up, she straddled him as she looked at him.

"How do you feel about having another person in our lives, say about seven months from now?"

Gregory just looked dumbfounded at her. She saw some tears gather in his eyes as one traveled down his face. Reaching up to his cheek, Samantha wiped his tear away as she smiled thru her own tears.

"Really Sam?" Shaking her head yes, Gregory touched her stomach and leaned forward to kiss it. That beautiful moment made her start to cry all over again.

"I love you Sam, more than my own life. How do you feel? Is that anything I can do for you right now?"

"I think you did enough already," giggled Samantha. "I have a doctor's appointment on Friday morning for us to go to."

"I wouldn't miss it for the world; let's wait to tell my folks and your Aunt until we know more."

Holding Samantha's hands to his lips, he gave them a kiss.

"I'm sorry about that image in the paper. I can't imagine how you felt when you saw it." Placing her fingers to his lips, she gave him a little smile. Samantha didn't want to think about it any longer.

"Let's go home so we can continue making up together." Linking her hand with his, Samantha locked up her Aunt's house and looked forward to spending the rest of the day and night with her husband.

Chapter 26 The Doctor's

On Friday morning, Gregory drove them to the doctors to find out what they needed to know about Samantha's pregnancy. Dr. Barbara Jones was one of Boston's leading prenatal doctors as

Gregory wanted to ensure that Samantha would be in good hands during her pregnancy.

"Do you want to know what we are having Sam? I'll only want to know if you do," Gregory said. He was so excited at becoming a Dad with Sam. He imagined that if they had a little girl that looked like Sam, she wouldn't date until she was 21. Gregory chuckled at that thought. Or how about a boy that looked like him. Maybe he would be strong in sports like Gregory was growing up or maybe take over the company after getting an MBA. Samantha looked over at her happy looking husband right now and had to ask him.

"Are you thinking about what we are having and what they would be when they grow up?" Samantha smiled up at him while holding his hand.

"Yeah, thinking if we have a girl, I won't let her date until she is 21 and if a boy, someone to take over our company."

"How about just a happy and healthy baby with whatever they want to be when they grow up. But I don't want to know what we are having. That is half the fun during labor, working towards that end result."

"Ok Mama, whatever you say," said Gregory. He realized he could never say no to anything to Sam asked of him.

Pulling into the doctor's parking lot, he escorted Sam in and got all of the paperwork set for her. It was his nervous energy that put her a little on edge as she took the paperwork from him to fill out herself. It would go faster that way.

Being called into the examining room, Samantha changed into a gown as they both waited for Dr. Jones to come in. They didn't have long to wait.

"Hello Mr. and Mrs. Steele, I'm Dr. Jones. It's so nice to meet the both of you." Getting the formalities out of the way, Dr. Jones explained what they were going to do today. As Samantha was on the examining table, Gregory held her hand and they both looked at the monitor together.

"Ok Samantha and Gregory. You are almost two months pregnant. I'm estimating that you became pregnant the beginning of June. Would that be about right?"

Gregory started smiling as Samantha started blushing. Samantha was right. It was the first time they slept together.

"I guess that's a yes," said Dr. Jones. Hearing the heartbeat, Samantha got tears in her eyes. Lately, she cried at the most silliest things: commercials, movies, even the sunsets from their apartment. Gregory commented about that to Dr. Jones.

"During the beginning of the pregnancy, hormones are constantly changing to also effect emotions, sleeping patterns, food cravings. You just have to go with it. It's certainly nothing to be concerned over." Checking to make sure all was perfect, Dr. Jones had Samantha sit up and relax. "Your baby is due anytime from March 1-8, somewhere within that time frame. Will you want to know the sex of the baby?"

Samantha said no at the same time Gregory said yes. "I can't help myself," said Gregory with a big smile on his face. Samantha rolled her eyes at him.

"I'll leave that for our next appointment then. I'll give you a prescription for pre-natal vitamins, instruction booklet and recommend a few books to read. You will feel queasy and tired this trimester but then it will pass and you will feel wonderful. We'll go thru the stages when we have our appointments. And yes, you can continue with intercourse. It's ok just as long as Samantha feels fine. If you have any questions, please call me. Just be kind to yourself during this time and get plenty of rest." Thanking Dr. Jones, Samantha got dressed so they could get ready to leave. Bending down to her belly, Gregory placed a kiss on it.

"I love you already little guy." Samantha put her hand thru Gregory's hair. Standing up next to her, Gregory cupped her face in his hands. "I love you, so very much Sam. You know we have to tell my folks and your Aunt now. We can tell Michael and Ronni tonight at the party."

Agreeing that it was as good a time as any, Samantha and Gregory called them from the car ride home to let them know the news. Putting them on speaker phone, they called his parents first. .

Diana started crying and James was yelling congratulations.

"You're a chip off the old block Greg!"

"Thanks Pop," laughed Gregory.

"How are you feeling Sam?"

"I'm feeling tired and a little queasy. The doctor assured me that this stage will pass," Samantha said.

"Just keep crackers and Ginger Ale with you and you'll be fine. We can't wait to see the both of you," said his parents as they hung up. Now Aunt Elaine was next one to call. This news had her Aunt crying tears of happiness for them. "I'll see you both tonight so I can properly congratulate you," said Aunt Elaine.

Hanging up the phone with her Aunt, Gregory looked over at Samantha. They just had pulled into their parking space when Gregory turned off the car. Looking over at her, he had to say what was on his mind.

"You know, never in my dreams did I think I would become a Father. My business consumed me that I didn't even think about settling down with anyone to even have a family. You have made me the happiest man on the planet Sam. I know that sounds ridiculous but I can't believe all of this."

Smiling over at Gregory, she agreed with him. "I'm also scared Gregory. A lot of changes in a short time and to become a mom now too; I have to let it all sink in."

"We'll get thru all of this together, all the fears and the happiness. We do have about two hours to get ready for the party too. Why don't you start to get ready and then relax? Do you need anything?"

Licking her bottom lip, Samantha just smiled over at him.

"Ok Mrs. Steele. We can be a little late to our party if we have to."

Chapter 27 Party

Stepping out from the bathroom, Samantha stood in front of the mirror to check out how she looked. Hair pulled up in sections with some pieces hanging down her back, the black gown fit perfectly with a generous cleavage showing to perfection. The dress had a little train behind it. She looked elegant and so far felt good.

"You need a few things for this dress," remarked Gregory. He was standing there looking so handsome in his tuxedo that her heart skipped a few beats.

Opening the jewelry case, Gregory brought out the sapphire and diamond necklace and placed it around her neck.

"This is beautiful Gregory." Samantha just touched the necklace while looking at her reflection in the mirror. He helped her with the diamond tennis bracelet too, one of her favorites.

"There you go," said Gregory. "You are gorgeous Sam."

"So are you, thank you," said Samantha. Looking at Gregory standing next to her in his tux, he looked so sexy.

Picking up her clutch, she linked her arm thru her handsome husband's and went to meet their driver. On the drive to the restaurant, Gregory held Samantha's hand and just stared at her. He couldn't believe how fortunate he was to be married to this incredible woman. He couldn't wait for his business associates to meet her and hoped that she would feel well enough to get thru the evening. Arriving before any of their guests, The Font de Riviera was an exclusive venue. Right on the water, the views were beautiful and the food had a five star rating.

It's the perfect place to celebrate our wedding and Gregory's business venture thought Samantha.

Paul and his partner Charlie were the first to arrive. Both looking dapper in their tuxes, Paul would be on call for whatever Gregory might need at the party. Taking Paul aside, Samantha thanked him for yesterday.

"No thanks are necessary Mrs. Steele. I knew Gregory would never do anything like that to you; it was too ridiculous to even think about. I had a feeling you would head over to your Aunt's and wanted to let her know what was going on."

"She surprised me as I had no idea that she owns the paper. When she called the editor, she ripped him apart," smiled Samantha."

"Your Aunt has a way about her, that's why I always tried to stay on her good side," said Paul. "Now go and enjoy your evening. I see your husband shooting daggers at me with his eyes."

Kissing Paul's cheek and holding Charlie's hand for a second, Samantha went to join Gregory to greet the rest of their guests. Ronni and Mike came in next. She looked amazing in little black dress with the low cut back and somewhat low cut front.

"I told Ronni that she shouldn't pay full price for that dress as half of it is missing," laughed Mike.

"Oh but you love it sweetheart!" purred Ronni.

"You got me there, "smiled Mike. He gave her a quick kiss and squeezed her hand.

"Would you ladies care for anything to drink?"

"Vodka and Cranberry for me," said Ronni

"Ginger Ale for me," said Samantha. Mike just stared at her.

"Really Sam?"

"You will be an Uncle in March," Samantha told him.

Hugging her and then slapping his brother on the back, Mike couldn't be happier.

"I knew it. This is wonderful news! Did you tell the folks?"

"Yes, today. We wanted to tell you here." Taking Mike aside, Gregory talked to him quickly.

"I told Dad about the contract, rip it up. He was furious. We don't need that ridiculous thing anymore."

"I know. He called me. I felt ten years old again like when we threw tomatoes at old Miss Connor's front porch and we couldn't sit down for a day," said Mike laughing.

Ronni and Samantha watched their handsome counterparts.

"He sure does look like Robert Redford," giggled Ronni.

Soon a steady throng of guests started coming in, including Aunt

Elaine and her date for the evening. Hugging Samantha, she was so happy that everything was turning out just the way it should for her. She was looking forward to being a Great-Aunt to the little one.

Carlotta came breezing in with her date for the evening.

Guessing that Samantha was pregnant, she whispered I told you so into her ear.

Standing next to Gregory, Samantha met all of his business partners. It was a long night for her but she kept up a conversation with everyone and they were just taken aback at how lovely she was and how attentive Gregory was to her. Excusing herself to get something to eat and drink, she leaned against the wall drinking her ginger ale.

"So you are Mrs. Gregory Steele, I'd like to introduce myself. I'm Alexandra Whitley, Gregory's fiancée," Alex said.

"You mean Ex-fiancée," informed Samantha.

"Don't you think it's all sudden, Gregory marrying you after a short courtship?" Alex tried to make Samantha insecure with her question but it wasn't having the effect that she wanted.

"After what you did, Gregory knew a good woman when he met me. Now, how did you get in here?"

"Well, Gregory invited me of course. He wanted to pick up where we left off the other night when I saw him with his business associates. We had shared quite a lot of each other over the past few years; of course he would want to be with me again."

Not taking the bait that Alexandra was saying, Samantha knew she had to get her out of party and quickly as to not cause attention to what was going on.

"I guess you didn't get a chance to read the paper this morning Alexandra," stated Samantha. "The writer and photographer retracted the story and apologized for making it looked like an affair when in turn it was just you getting your ass thrown out of the restaurant. Now, I don't know how you got in here, but this is an invitation only party and you certainly would not qualify to be on the guest list," said Samantha.

Gregory saw the confrontation from across the room and headed over to Samantha with Michael and Ronni right with him. Hearing the last part of what Samantha said to Alex, Gregory stepped next to Samantha to confront her.

"My wife is right Alex. How in the hell did you get in here?" Gregory stood right next to Samantha for additional support.

"I am the guest of someone who was invited," Alex said.

"Sorry, not good enough, I'm asking you to leave immediately and never come near my wife or myself ever again, do I make myself clear?" Alex knew at that moment, that Gregory was lost forever to her. Paul came over to Gregory's side.

"Can I be of assistance Mr. Steele?"

"Alex seems to have forgotten who escorted her to this party so I need her escorted out of here immediately. Please see to that

Paul."

"Yes Sir," Paul said. "Ms. Whitley, this way please." Samantha noticed that Paul put the emphasis on Ms. Lifting her head, she walked out of the restaurant area without anyone knowing that something was wrong. One thing with Alexandra Whitley, she didn't want any negative publicity connected with her name and she would have gotten that is this instance. Samantha would have seen to that.

Gregory cued up the orchestra to play something everyone could dance to.

"May I have this dance my love?"

Placing her hand in his, they enjoyed the music that the band was playing. Gregory couldn't believe how very lucky he was and how very happy he would make Samantha.

"Care to join me with this dance Ronni?" Mike bowed in front of her. Ronni started giggling at him.

"Absolutely, "said Ronni. She gave him a radiant smile as she looked up at him. Mike guided her to the floor as both brothers gracefully danced their ladies across the room.

"You make this look real good Mike. I didn't know you and Gregory could dance like this," Ronni said.

"Actually Dad taught us, he's quite the dancer himself. How do you think he got my mom to marry him?" Pulling Ronni closer to him, he felt the open back of her dress and how much skin was exposed.

She was driving him crazy with wanting her but he dare not try anything, not yet anyway. He knew he loved Ronni or was definitely on his way to doing so. The analytical lawyer mind kept weighing both sides of getting into a serious relationship. He was working on forgetting the first betrayal from his former fiancée but knew he could be in a very happy, crazy and loving relationship with Ronni but just wanted to take things slow. So he kept things on safe topics like becoming an Uncle.

"You will be an amazing Uncle," Ronni said. Looking over at Gregory and Sam, she was so happy that her friend found love. "They look so happy."

"You make me happy too Ronni," Mike said. He leaned down to brush her lips with his. Smiling up at him, he finished up the dance with a little dip before escorting her off the dance floor. As the party was coming to a close, reporters finished their photos. Going thru guest names with Samantha, she gave approval for which magazines they wanted the photos to be featured in. With that business at hand all taken care of, Gregory gathered his wife and saying goodbye to anyone staying, they headed home with their driver. Safely tucked into the car, Samantha leaned against the back seat and sighed.

"What a beautiful night Gregory," Samantha said. "Congratulations on the merger. I know this is what you wanted."

"Congratulations to us Sam," Gregory said. "I couldn't have done this without you."

Chapter 28 It's time

Across town, Mike was driving Ronni to her apartment. Pulling up in front, Ronni sat there contemplating her next move. She knew that Mike was the one for her, she was certain of it. Right from the moment he scared her in front of the refrigerator, she knew that she had to get to know him. No other man had ever reached out to her soul like he has but she didn't know how to be with him knowing what his former fiancée did to him. He wasn't really making any moves to take their relationship to the next level so she thought she would have to be the first to do it and see what happens.

"Would you like to come up with me? You can park next to my car for guests if you do." She held her breath, not knowing what Mike would say to her. He decided to be blunt with her.

"If I come upstairs with you Ronni, it isn't to hold hands. Do you understand that?" Looking straight at Mike, she nodded back at him. This was one time a sassy comeback would have been inappropriate and besides, she wanted to be with him.

Parking the car, he came around to open her door to help her out. Letting them into the main lobby, they stood side by side, waiting for the elevator to get there. Stepping in, Mike pulled her close to him and ravaged her mouth making her whimper with her need of him. His hand moved under her dress and cupped her buttocks, pulling her closer to him. As the elevator slowed to her floor, they rearranged their clothes just in case someone was waiting when the door opened.

"What is it about elevators that make people do that?"

"It's the danger of being caught," remarked Ronni.

Letting them into her apartment, she asked him if he wanted something to drink. Grabbing a beer for him, she decided on a glass of wine for herself.

"I'll be right back. Please make yourself comfortable," Ronni said.

Mike sat on the couch, looking down at his beer. His emotions were all over the place; from really caring about Ronni to the betrayal he went thru months earlier. Ronni could be someone he could spend the rest of his life with, his mind was spinning with doubts and also with the need of being with her. He had to put the broken engagement and the betrayal of his former fiancé behind him. It was time. Ronni wasn't anything like her and wasn't the type of woman to be dishonest with him or anyone.

"Mike," whispered Ronni. Standing at the door was a beautiful sight. In a sheer teddy that left nothing to the imagination, Ronni was offering herself to him. Putting his beer down, he kicked his shoes off as he loosened up his tie. Coming over to her, he didn't realize how petite she was and that a wave of wanting to protect her came over him.

With her hands slightly shaking, Ronni took off his tie while looking deep into his eyes. She started to unbutton his shirt and pulled it out of his pants. Moving her hands thru his blond chest hair, she brushed his shirt off his shoulders to the floor. She slowly unbuckled his belt and pushed his pants down the length of him. He was gorgeous. Muscles rippling in anticipation, Mike picked her up and laid her gently on her bed. Looking into her green eyes, he smiled down at her. She knew that this moment was the way it was supposed to be. She pulled his head to hers for a kiss that ignited into a rapidly burning flame. Pushing her teddy up over her head, Mike whispered how beautiful she was. Moving his mouth to her breasts, her nipples rose in response to what he was doing to her. His hand slowly descended inside her panties where Mike felt she was ready for him. Pulling off her panties and then his briefs, Ronni saw Mike's erection with hunger in her eyes. Smiling down at Ronni, he knelt between her legs and started kissing her, teasing her. Straining her hips upwards towards Mike, he knew that his girl loved this part of love making as much as he loved doing it. Ronni was crying out with the need to feel Mike inside her. Teasing her with his mouth, his tongue kissed every inch of her. He couldn't get enough of her as his tongue dipped inside of her as Ronni pulled his head closer into her. Moving to her clit, he drove her to an earth shattering climax that took her breath away.

Kissing his way back up her body, he kissed her lips so she tasted herself on him. He slowly started entering her and stopped.

"Ronni, what the Hell?"

"Please Mike; I want it to be with you. Please," begged Ronni.

"I don't think I could stop now if I tried," answered Mike. Leaning forward to kiss her, he thrust past the barrier that made her a woman. Waiting a moment for her to adjust to him, she raised her hips instinctively wanting more of him. Mike started moving within her as her moans drove him crazy. He wanted to show her how wonderful loving her can be. Ronni needed him and felt herself being drawn higher with him as his movements increased until suddenly, she felt a beautiful release that Mike gave her. Crying out his name, Mike wanted it to be good for her. Feeling her tighten around him, he joined her towards a sweet ending that only Ronni could give him. As they started to relax, Ronni reached up to touch Mike's face and brushed his hair off his forehead.

"How and why?"

The attorney in him started coming out.

"How is that we seduced each other and it happened. Why is because I've waited for a special man like you to come into my life and wanted it to be with you. That's why," Ronni said.

Rolling to his side, he pulled Ronni with him.

"You amaze me. I would have never thought that you would be a virgin."

"I've done other things before but obviously not this."

Looking at her, Mike knew in his heart this was the woman for him and he would never let her go.

"Come here, "said Mike.

"Absolutely," replied Ronni.

Across town, Samantha was exhausted beyond belief. Gregory tucked her in bed with a kiss on her forehead. All thoughts of making love to her tonight stopped as he saw the dark circles under her eyes. Her eyes were closing shut before he could even saw goodnight to her. There would be plenty of time for loving her another day.

Getting in on his side of the bed, he pulled her close to him and fell fast asleep.

Chapter 29 The Fair

Rolling over in bed, Samantha reached for Gregory but grabbed an empty pillow instead. Then she smelled bacon cooking from the kitchen and smiled knowing he was making them breakfast. When her cell phone started ringing, she reached over to it and saw that it was Ronni calling her.

"Hey Ronni. How are you?"

"Well I did it," Ronni said.

"Did what? Oh that. Really, with Mike?"

Chatting a few minutes together as there was nothing like good girl talk, Ronni mentioned that they were going to the fair in the afternoon and wanted to know if they wanted to join them.

"Might be fun, I'll speak to Gregory and get back to you."

Hanging up with her, Gregory was on his cell phone with Mike.

"Really, oh really," Gregory said. "Sure, the fair sounds great. I'll check with Sam and get back to you.

Hearing that, Samantha yelled out to Gregory that yes, we'll go.

"The little Mama said yes Mike. We'll talk more when I see you."

Hanging up with him, Gregory came into the bedroom to find his naked wife lying in bed.

"Last night, I believe you wanted something from me that I was too tired to give to you," Samantha said. Reaching out to Gregory, all thoughts of breakfast left his mind. Her hormones being out of whack gave her such a sexual appetite that she basically attacked Gregory. He certainly didn't have any complaints about that. Pulling him down, she straddled on top of him with a big sigh. Smiling up at his gorgeous wife, Gregory grabbed hold of her hips and started moving in and out of her. Moving one hand to her breast, he pulled on her nipples as she cried out in pleasure as her breasts were much more sensitive than usual. Feeling her tighten already, he couldn't believe that Sam was going to come so quickly.

"Oh Gregory, I'm near."

"Go on Sam, there are plenty where this is coming from today," smiled Gregory. He just wanted to give his wife pleasure as he moved his fingers to her clit. That did it for Samantha as she felt herself come apart at his touch. As she slowed down, Gregory moved her to her back without losing connection to her. Moving her legs around his hips, he was able to move deeper into her as she moaned deep in her throat.

"Gregory, harder please." Thinking that he loved this new Sam, he gave her what she wanted. Getting totally lost with how good she felt, Gregory slammed deeper inside of her that she bucked off the bed when her second orgasm hit her hard. As he grew harder within her, he knew he was near. Feeling Samantha build up again, Gregory felt an incredible rush go thru him as he surrendered himself to these feelings. Samantha joined him as they both climaxed together as Gregory collapsed on top of her.

"If pregnancy does this to you, I'm a dead man," chuckled Gregory. "I promise to have the first round on top of you so you can save your energy for the rest." Looking at the time, they each took showers to get ready to go to the fair.

Meeting Ronni and Mike at the fair was exactly what Samantha needed. It was a beautiful summer afternoon with fresh air that put color back in Samantha's cheeks. Ronni was being her outrageous self that she had Samantha laughing as usual. Linking her arm thru Samantha's, she wanted to talk to her about what happened with her and Mike.

"It was exactly what I imagined Sam," Ronni said. She was glowing with happiness as she spoke about Mike. That wasn't lost on

Samantha. "He was shocked at first; I guess any man would be because of my age."

"I think it also has to do with your crazy personality, your fun, flirty ways with men that one would have never known. Was he good with you?"

"Oh yeah, I wore him out!"

"You are too much," laughed Samantha.

Walking behind the girls, Mike and Gregory were having a similar conversation.

"I was surprised, that's all Greg," explained Mike.

"I'm sure you took care of her Mike," Gregory said.

"Actually, she wore me out," laughed Mike.

"You don't look worse for the wear," laughed Gregory. "Well, we both have our hands full, don't we?"

"Yeah and I like it," Mike said.

Walking thru the fair, the guys won teddy bears for the girls. There was an arts and crafts section where the local artisans sold their goods. Samantha picked up a beautiful crochet baby blanket and Ronni picked up a few decorative pillows for her couch. The guys bought them all ice cream to cool off a bit in the heat. After enjoying a nice afternoon with Ronni and Mike, Samantha was ready to head home to get some rest.

"The doctor said I'll feel better in a few weeks. Until then, I'm sorry to call it a day," Samantha said. Putting his arm around his wife, he gave her a kiss on her cheek.

"We'll catch up with you guys during the week. I'm going to get the little Mama home," said Gregory.

Saying their goodbyes, Mike wanted to stay with Ronni and had his mind on other things for them to do. Holding her hand, he pulled her close to him.

"What do you say we go back to my place and we order dinner in?"

"I would love that but can think of other things to do before ordering dinner in," said Ronni seductively.

"Well lead the way Ms. Tate. I think I have woken up a sleeping giant," Mike said. Reaching Mike's Corvette, he helped her into his car. As he went to step back, she grabbed the front of his tee-shirt and pulled him down to her for a kiss that showed him what she wanted to be doing with him. "Don't start anything you can't finish right now Ronni," said Mike. Touching her cheek, he moved his hand down the front of her shirt while lightly touching her breast. He smiled at the response he got from Ronni.

"Hold that thought, we'll be at my house in ten minutes."

Jumping in the driver's side, Mike maneuvered the Corvette in and out of traffic.

"You are quiet Ronni," commented Mike.

"I'm thinking about the things I am going to do to you," answered Ronni.

"You do speak your mind," replied Mike.

Getting to his apartment in what was record time, Mike helped
Ronni out of the Corvette and up to his place. Entering the spacious
apartment, Ronni loved to open layout of his loft. For a brief
second, she wondered how many women he brought here as she
looked around.

"Could you point me in the direction of the bathroom so I can
freshen up?"

"Sure, down the hall to the left. There are fresh towels in the linen
closet in the bathroom."

Walking towards the bathroom, Ronni pulled off her tee-shirt and
let it drop to the floor.

"Would you care to join me Mike?"

"What do you think," said a smiling Mike. Grabbing some condoms
from his bedroom night stand while on his way to the bathroom,
Mike found Ronni filling up the bathtub while in her bra and
panties. Coming up behind her, Mike wrapped his arms around her
waist and pulled her up against him. One hand started caressing
her breast while the other hand sought the place between her legs.
Leaning against him, Ronni's newly found senses were craving the
release that only Mike could satisfy within her. Reaching into her
panties, Mike found the spot that gave Ronni the most pleasure and
drove her wild with wanting him. He wanted to show her all the
different ways of loving her and he knew she was a willing student.
Feeling herself building up for a release, she reached behind her and

moved her hand against Mike's erection. Not wanting to be distracted from pleasuring Ronni, he grabbed her hand away from him and held it against her body. While his fingers plunged deep within her, his mouth caressed her neck. Ronni moaned out Mike's name as she felt her release building within her. Throwing her head back against him, Ronni was certain she would pass out from his assault on her senses. Releasing her hand, Mike made his way up to her breasts, touching them the way she loved him too. Feeling Ronni tighten around his fingers, Mike moved them faster and deeper within her until she cried out his name in her release. Turning in his arms, she sought out his mouth and just melted against him. She never thought that these feelings were possible. Reaching down to touch him, Ronni wanted nothing more than to give Mike the same pleasure.

Stepping into the bathtub, she held out her hand to Mike and helped him to sit down. Straddling him, Ronni lowered herself onto his rock hard erection.

"You are so tight there," Mike breathed. Ronni gave him a wink and a smile and started the age old movements that only women know what to do. As Mike got caught up with what Ronni was doing to him, all thoughts of condoms went out the window. While she moved seductively on top of him, Mike leaned forward to cup her buttocks to bring her down closer on him while his mouth sucked on her nipples. That was Ronni's undoing as she called out Mike's name in pleasure while moving faster on top of him to bring Mike to his release. Feeling him getting bigger inside of her, Mike grabbed her hair and pulled her mouth to his.

"Oh Ronni, I love you," Mike moaned. He felt himself rush into her. As things quieted down between them, Ronni kissed his cheeks, chin, forehead and then his mouth.

"I love you too Mike." Ronni kissed him long and hard on his mouth. Slowly moving off of him, she lay cradled in his arm, while she played with the blond hair on his chest. Mike slicked back his hair from his face and looked down at her.

"Let's get out of here. Are you hungry?"

"For you, always," Ronni said.

Dinner was all but forgotten as Mike and Ronni spent the evening exploring each other.

Mike woke up Monday morning to a note that Ronni left him.

"Sorry to leave without waking you but you seem to need your beauty rest after last night. I'll come by for lunch today around one o'clock. I'll be able to get away at that time. I love you. R"

Mike smiled at her note. Enjoying his new relationship, Mike realized how fortunate he was to have met her. On top of that, she was an amazing lover for it being a new thing for her. She gave him a gift that he will always treasure. This could very well be someone that he could share his life with. Looking at the time, Mike sent her a quick text and then sent one to his secretary to clear his schedule from

1-2:30 for a lunch date.

Smiling, Mike jumped into the shower to start his day.

Chapter 30 The Lunch Date

The morning over at Crescendo Steele Publishing went by fast for Samantha and Ronni. They had meetings together with Gregory to figure out a game plan for Carlotta's European tour. With the Italian firm merger, getting them on a conference call with promises of pushing Carlotta's novel in that region as well as other suggestions set them on the path to a successful tour for her.

"I'll get Carlotta up to speed with these ideas," Samantha said. "I'm sure she will be receptive to any and all plans we have for her."

"That's great Sam," Gregory said. "I'll leave this in your capable hands. Ronni, I'll just need those figures from you for her sales today."

"Not a problem Gregory. I'll email you everything after lunch," Ronni said.

"Thank you," said Gregory. "Speaking of lunch, would my lovely wife care to join me?"

"Of course," Samantha smiled. She was starting to feel better in her pregnancy that she gained some of her appetite back.

"If you don't need me for anything else right now, I'll see the both of you after lunch," Ronni said.

"We are set Ronni," Gregory said.

Watching her leave the office, Gregory turned to Samantha.

"I wonder what her hurry is. She hardly sat still the last half hour of our meeting and kept looking at her watch," Gregory said.

"For such a smart man, you can be so oblivious at times. I think she has a lunch date with your brother," smiled Samantha. "Things are getting pretty serious between them."

"Well, that makes sense then," Gregory said. "I may be oblivious at times with others, but never with you my love. Let's go back to our café where this all started."

"I would love that Gregory." Taking her hand in his, they walked thru the office with the staff smiling at the both of them.

Looking at the time on the other side of town, Michael was counting the minutes to when he could expect Ronni for their lunch date. Hearing a commotion at this door, he saw his secretary try to stop a woman who was determined on seeing Michael.

"I'm sorry Mr. Steele but she just barged past me."

"It's ok Madeline, I'll handle this."

Looking at his ex fiancé, Mike sat back in his chair. Watching her walk into his office with narrowed eyes, he couldn't help but feel disgust towards her.

"What do you want Jessica?"

"Well, you of course. All I think about is you and now that my divorce is final, I'm hoping that we could pick up where we left off," Jessica said. She walked to the front of his desk and sat on the corner of it. Mike looked at her long, shapely legs and full breasts in the form fitting blouse. All he could think about was how cheap looking Jessica was, especially compared to his lovely Ronni.

"Well you thought wrong Jessica," Mike said. "You have wasted a trip coming down her to see me." Coming around his desk, he took her arm and pulled her off his desk. Not wanting to miss her chance, Jessica leaned her body into his and put her arms up around his neck. Mike took his hands and removed her arms from around his neck and held her away from him.

"It's done Jessica. I've moved on and I would suggest you do so too," advised Mike. Reaching up to his face, she tried to trace his lips with her fingers as Mike grabbed her wrist in a vice like grip.

"Excuse me but am I interrupting something?" Ronni stood in the doorway, witnessing everything in front of her. Feeling her heart breaking, she turned and headed back down the hallway as fast as she could.

"Ronni, please wait!" Yelling for his secretary, Madeline showed up in his doorway.

"Please see to it that Jessica is removed by security and never allowed back into this building." Moving past both women, he ran down the hallway to get Ronni but the elevator door closed as he soon as he got there.

"Ronni, wait!" Mike shouted. Slamming the elevator door with his fist, Mike went back to his office as security was escorting Jessica down the hallway.

"Don't you ever come back here or around me ever again, do I make myself clear?"

Shaking her head in agreement, Jessica knew it was completely done and nothing could change that fact. Stepping into the elevator, Jessica stepped out of Mike's life for the last time.

Mike left several messages for Ronni at work and on her cell to no avail. He decided to give Samantha a call. Explaining everything that had happened, Mike asked Samantha where she could be.

"I have to explain everything to her Sam. I can't lose her over this," Mike said. Hearing the desperation in his voice, Samantha was certain he was in love with Ronni and she would do everything she could to help him.

"I'll help you find Ronni. Don't worry," Samantha said. Hanging up with him, Samantha told Cindy she would be gone for the rest of the afternoon and then went in search for her husband. Finding him in his office, Samantha quickly told him what had transpired in Mike's office with Jessica and that Ronni witnessed Mike in Jessica's embrace.

"That woman is a bitch," Gregory said. "And you think Mike is in love with Ronni?"

"I'm sure of it," answered Samantha.

"Then let's help my brother find your friend," answered Gregory.

After asking Paul to handle the afternoon for him and to alert them if Ms. Tate returns to the office, they went to help locate her.

"Ok, where do you think she is?"

"Let's try the yoga studio first," Samantha said. Gregory pulled the Maserati out of his parking spot and headed downtown. Calling Mike along the way, Samantha told him they would do their best to help him.

"I love Ronni, Samantha. I have to find her and explain everything," Mike said.

"It will be fine Mike, we'll help where we can," Gregory replied. Hanging up with Mike, Gregory and Samantha knew they had to help his brother.

Not finding her at the yoga studio, Samantha was thinking about their next move when Aunt Elaine called her.

"Are you looking for someone?"

"Is Ronni with you?" Samantha hoped her Aunt would tell her Ronni was with her.

"Yes. Why don't the three of you come over here and then Mike can speak with her while the three of us visit," Aunt Elaine said.

"Is she ok?"

"Ronni is upset but I think she will be fine. She loves him and with time, Ronni will understand what happened. They just have to talk about it."

Calling Mike on his cell, Samantha told him that Ronni was with her Aunt.

"Mike, she is at my Aunt's house. We'll meet you there," Samantha said.

After giving Mike her Aunt's address, she hung up her cell.

Samantha reached for Gregory's hand. Grateful at how their relationship was, she wished that for Ronni and Mike too.

"I love you Gregory," smiled Samantha. He squeezed her hand and then touched her belly.

"I love you and our baby," answered Gregory. "Let's go help my brother."

Heading across town, they arrived at Aunt Elaine's house before Mike.

After hugging her Aunt, she told Samantha that Ronni was in the garden.

Stepping outside in the peaceful haven, Samantha found her in the corner sitting on a bench crying.

"Hey Ronni," Samantha said. Reaching out to hug Ronni, she heard her crying. It broke Samantha's heart to see her friend hurting when she knew there was an explanation to what had happened.

"Hey," Ronni said. She looked at Samantha while wiping the tears from her eyes. "Did anyone say that love hurts?"

"Of course, that's why it's so worth it," Samantha said. Taking Ronni's hand in hers, she gave it a squeeze. "You know Ronni, Mike loves you. He told Gregory and me this on our way here. He's on his way here too so he can talk to you," Samantha said. "He's so afraid he is going to lose you, so please at least give him a chance."

"I love him too, I gave myself to him and then I see this woman all over him. I joke about a lot of things but that just shocked me," Ronni said. "I love him Sam but can't help feeling betrayed."

"Just give him a chance, ok?"

"Yes, I will," Ronni said.

"Good Ronni, as I need you to listen to me," Mike said. Mike stood there, looking as upset as Ronni was. Looking at Mike, Ronni was relieved that he came by to talk.

"I'll be right inside if you need me," Samantha said. Giving Ronni a kiss on her cheek, she passed by Mike and gave his arm a squeeze.

She noticed Gregory waiting for her on the patio and went up there to meet him. Taking her hand, Gregory went inside with Samantha to wait with her Aunt.

"May I sit down?"

Nodding her head yes, Mike sat down and reached up to wipe the tears from her cheeks.

"Ronni, what you saw in my office was a desperate, selfish woman attempting to pick up where our relationship ended just as I was having her removed from the building." Turning her by her shoulders to face him, he gently touched her chin to lift her face to his.

"I didn't know what to think when I saw her all over you Mike. After all that we have shared, I didn't think I was enough for you, that maybe you wanted someone with more experience than what I have."

"Ronni, it's you that I love, you that make all the difference in my world. It's you that I want to spend the rest of my life with, have children with. Without you, I am nothing. I need you to understand this. What you saw meant nothing to me. If I don't have you in my life, I don't know what I would do."

Ronni looked him with tears in her eyes.

"Marry me," Ronni demanded.

A slow smile parted his lips. Of course she would be the one in their relationship that would do the asking.

"Yes, I will," Mike said. Lowering his mouth to hers, Mike sealed their agreement with a kiss, one that would bind them together with a promise of love for the rest of their lives.

Chapter 31 Wedding

Two months later, Ronni and Mike stood at the water's edge at sunset, pledging their love to each other. With Samantha and Gregory by their side as witnesses, it was an intimate gathering of family and a few friends. James and Diana were present as they had missed Gregory's wedding and didn't want to miss their other son's wedding day.

"I now pronounce you Man and Wife. You may kiss your Bride."

"Absolutely," smiled Mike. He started to pull Ronni in closer for a kiss but she whispered something in his ear.

"I'm having your baby."

"Really? Did it happen on our first night?"

"Most likely," Ronni said. She looked so beautiful smiling up at him with tears in her eyes.

Gregory stood next to his brother and gave him a little nudge.

"Are you kissing your Bride anytime soon?"

"I'm getting around to it but she just told me she's pregnant!"

Cheers went up with Samantha hugging her dear friend. James and Diana couldn't believe they will have two grandchildren by next year.

Gregory hugged his brother with tears of happiness in his eyes. He realized how very blessed they all were and how so many wonderful changes happened in their lives.

"Excuse me," said the Judge. "Mike, you have forgotten one thing."

"Yes your Honor," said Mike. He wrapped his arms around Ronni.

"I may now kiss my Bride."

Epilogue

"Samantha and Gregory, you have a beautiful baby boy!"

Samantha started crying at hearing the news that they had a son. Gregory had tears in his eyes too as he bent over to give his wife a kiss.

"Thank you Sam. You will be an amazing Mom for our son. I love you so much."

Gregory looked up as the doctor was handing him his son, who was definitely letting the world know he had arrived. Bringing his son between him and Samantha, he asked her what she wanted to call him.

"I was thinking James Thomas Steele, after your Dad and mine. "

Touching her son's face and then holding his little hand, Samantha thought their son was just so perfect. Gregory looked down at her, with so much love that he never thought possible. Holding them both in his arms, he couldn't agree more about his name.

"It's a perfect name for him Sam," agreed Gregory.

Handing his son back to the doctor, Gregory kissed Samantha on the forehead and went to let family and friends know there is a new boy in the family. It was a new beginning for the Steele family and a new beginning in their lives.

Made in the USA
Middletown, DE
05 July 2016